FOREVER
Home

Forever Home ranks as one of the very best Amish love stories I've ever read. Amy Grochowski takes this genre of fiction in an enticing new direction. Her writing is—quite simply—fabulous. I could not put it down. If you love a writer who draws you into her story world and won't let you go until the happily ever after-Amy's the one for you.

—LAUREL BLOUNT,
Award-winning author of the *Love Inspired Pine Valley* series

I love everything about *Forever Home*—the characters, the relationships, the vivid imagery, and the refreshing plot twists. Not only is it a compelling love story, but author Amy Grochowski has thoughtfully interwoven the redemptive truth of God's love and forgiveness. I was drawn further into the story with each page and at the end found myself hoping for a sequel!

—DR. SHANNON WARDEn,
Counselor, professor, and co-author with Dr. Gary Chapman of
The DIY Guide to Building a Family That Lasts

Amish Dreams on Prince Edward Island
Book One

FOREVER
Home

AMY GROCHOWSKI

AMBASSADOR INTERNATIONAL
GREENVILLE, SOUTH CAROLINA & BELFAST, NORTHERN IRELAND

www.ambassador-international.com

Forever Home

Amish Dreams on Prince Edward Island, Book One
A Contemporary Amish Romance
© 2020 by Amy Grochowski
All rights reserved

ISBN: 978-1-62020-724-6
eISBN: 978-1-62020-743-7
Library of Congress Control Number: 2020938637

This is a work of fiction. Names, characters, and incidents are all products of the author's imagination or are used for fictional purposes. Any resemblance to actual events or persons, living or dead, is entirely coincidental. Any mentioned brand names, places, and trademarks remain the property of their respective owners, bear no association with the author or the publisher, and are used for fictional purposes only.

Cover Design & Typesetting by Hannah Nichols

AMBASSADOR INTERNATIONAL
Emerald House
411 University Ridge, Suite B14
Greenville, SC 29601, USA
www.ambassador-international.com

AMBASSADOR BOOKS
The Mount
2 Woodstock Link
Belfast, BT6 8DD, Northern Ireland, UK
www.ambassadormedia.co.uk

The colophon is a trademark of Ambassador, a Christian publishing company.

In memory of Elmer W. Day, my grandfather, who explained salvation so a child could understand.

And for my father, David N. Washburn Sr., who listened to my early desire for redemption and led me the rest of the way to my Savior.

My little children, I am writing these things to you so that you may not sin. But if anyone does sin, we have an advocate with the Father, Jesus Christ the righteous.

1 John 2:1

ACKNOWLEDGMENTS

To David, who partners with my every endeavor, for your endless patience and unwavering encouragement. Mom and Dad, for believing in me and for all the days and nights you kept the boys so I could write. Nathaniel and Timothy, for eating frozen pizzas and thinking Mom is cool even if she talks to imaginary people hidden in her laptop.

To all my family and friends, too numerous to name, who have prayed, encouraged, read, and dreamed alongside me. I owe you an enormous debt of gratitude.

To my editor, Katie Cruice Smith, for her eagle eye and enduring patience. I'm ever grateful for your dedicated work on this story.

To Jan Drexler and Tina Radcliff, for your time and generous instruction in the craft of inspirational writing. Your input has been invaluable. I continue to aspire to the bar you have set for excellence in Christian fiction.

To Sam Lowry, Anna Raats, and everyone at Ambassador International, for your support of *Forever Home* and efforts to share its message in print.

To Jesus, my Savior, Friend, and Counselor, if there is any praise for my work, I owe it all to You.

CHAPTER ONE

October, 2016

Lancaster County, Pennsylvania

A sensible Amish woman aspired to marry, as Lydia Miller was reminded daily.

She also knew any wise Amish woman ought to bypass schemes destined to failure. Yet here she stood, determined to avoid the first and ready to plunge headlong into the second.

Lydia sucked in a breath and slid into a seat on the second-to-last row of chairs under the auction tent. She may not win the bid for the farmhouse at today's estate sale, but at least she'd know she tried everything to keep her business.

The air smelled of autumn—the cooling rest of the earth after yielding her summer labor. Under the heavy canvas of the tent, the two-mile stretch of Amish farmland known as Millers Creek was hidden from Lydia's view.

A wet trickle of perspiration trailed from underneath her prayer *kapp,* then down the back of Lydia's neck. She almost allowed Ben to bid for her; but her brother wasn't familiar with her finances, nor was his future on the bidding block.

Nay, the task was up to her alone.

The wooden seat beside Lydia creaked under the heft of her neighbor, Miriam Stoltzfus, who emitted a groan of her own as she sat.

"Have you lost all of your good sense?"

Ever since Lydia's *mamm* died, Miriam had taken the mother role upon herself. Lydia was used to the older woman's more-often-than-not good intentions, which were more than Lydia needed at the moment. "I still have all my wits about me."

The click of Miriam's tongue against her teeth issued her contradiction. Lydia's vision settled onto the handle attached to her bidder card. The rounded edge of the re-purposed tongue depressor pressed into her palm. Lydia prayed a silent prayer of forgiveness for the unkind urge to use it on the other woman.

"*Gott's* will couldn't be plainer if Moses himself carved it on a stone tablet for you to read." Miriam's prayer *kapp* bobbed up and down with the surety of her conviction.

The Almighty's will? Or Miriam's? Lydia had to wonder.

Lydia shoved the tongue depressor between her knees for safe-keeping and pressed her lips tight to keep from disrespecting her elder, who continued in a not-so-quiet whisper. "The sale of this property—including your Amish Shoppe—is a clear sign the time has come for you to quit this spinster nonsense and settle down with a *goot* Amish husband."

"And marry whom?" *Not your cousin, Hiram Glick,* Lydia thought to herself. Miriam knew full well Lydia couldn't accept Hiram. "I could own a business, not just rent the building." Lydia turned to face her neighbor. "You know why this is important to me." She didn't dare say the reason aloud. Miriam was one of the few who knew the reason for her determination to support herself.

"*Ya,* I know. Even so, I tell you, Lydia, this is a mistake. The Lord has a bigger plan for you. He is not bound by the past. Remember, with *Gott* all things are possible."

"Well then, it's still possible I might buy this house and save my shop today."

Miriam sank with a deflated plop against the back of her seat.

Lydia had the last word, but satisfaction didn't follow. Miriam's words nagged at her conscience. Not the part about signs and plans. Lydia didn't believe she deserved such consideration. Rather, she was struck by the existence of a Power great enough to overcome the past. If only the past had not bound her.

But she was Lydia Miller, humble mortal.

Lydia shifted in her seat. She had attended many auctions, but never bid for anything. She bit her lower lip. Did she know what she was doing with such a large sum and stakes so high? All the money she had earned from five years of teaching in the Amish school had been poured into renovating the farmhouse into a shop. Now, she had only her business savings to try and outbid the fancy men here today.

Ouch. Lydia jumped from a sharp jab in the ribs.

"I wasn't talking about Hiram, if that's what you're thinking." Miriam aimed the offending finger toward an Amish man whom Lydia had never seen.

Tall with powerful strong shoulders, he stood alone on the far side of the tent, tapping his straw hat against his leg. The Amish stranger's face was tanned and his hair the blackest she'd ever seen. His dark eyes, set deep under thick brows, met her own. Lydia ducked her head, but not before she noticed his square, unshaven chin. Unmarried.

"What in the world?" Lydia leaned into Miriam to keep her voice low. "Now you'd try to match me with a man we don't even know?"

"He's Canadian Amish. Beulah Yoder's grandson."

"Oh . . . so, you'd have me marry the man responsible for this . . . " Lydia's throat tightened. If she attempted to describe what this horrible day really meant to her, she'd be in tears. She couldn't afford the distraction. As far as Lydia was concerned, the man should have stayed in Canada where he belonged. He hadn't been around these parts even when his grandmother was alive. All was fine and dandy if he wanted to sell his inheritance, but a little more notice would have been appreciated.

"Maybe he's a bit responsible, but . . . "

The auctioneer interrupted Miriam by calling for the first bid. Lydia jumped to join with the rest of the bidders. Was her eagerness too obvious? She wished her *datt* were still alive to give her advice.

The rumble of the first bids began like the intermittent thunder of a faraway storm. As the bidders increased, the fervor pitched faster and faster. Lydia sat on the edge of her chair as though lightning might strike her. All of a sudden, the bidding slowed. Several bidders had thinned to a few, and Lydia was amazed to find herself still alive among them.

She had better free her mind of distractions—the smell of the straw beneath her feet, the flap of the canvas roof above her . . . Focus, focus. Wasn't that what *Datt* used to say? Focus on the task at hand.

She concentrated on the auctioneer and an *Englischer* in the corner of her periphery. She'd met many non-Amish neighbors and businessmen since opening her shop, but she didn't recognize this one. Unlike the Amish stranger who watched with his jaw squared in concern, this man was relaxed as he upped the price time and again. He was confident about something, for sure. Was the auction a game to him?

Her pulse buzzed in her ears. This was her life, not an amusing way to pass the time.

The auctioneer looked at her. The third-to-last bidder must have bailed. Lydia lifted her card to an amount that squeezed every penny from her account. She had no collateral or credit for a loan. The bid had to be her last.

The man countered and waited. So smug.

She had rented the large farmhouse, remodeled it with her savings from five years as a teacher in the Amish school, and then turned it into a profitable business. Yet this man waltzed into her community to buy it right out from under her.

Lydia raised her number.

His expression remained unchanged. He bid again.

She'd go until she saw him sweat. Her card sailed into the air over and over again.

The Amish men began to murmur. The handsome Amish stranger was staring at her. With concern or admiration? She couldn't take time to wonder. She looked back at her opponent.

The *Englisch* bidder no longer slouched against the tent pole. He upped the price. And Lydia countered. The auctioneer's cadence carried across a room full of people gone silent.

Miriam grabbed Lydia's hand and squeezed hard enough to break every one of her fingers. If the man didn't bid, Lydia was in worse trouble than she'd thought possible from this day.

One last bid. Lydia held her breath. The cotton fabric of her apron pressed into her palms as she dried them. What would she do if he didn't go for it?

The man wiped perspiration from his forehead and raised his card.

"Going, going . . . gone."

The gavel dropped with a thud, and the echo of splintered dreams reverberated through Lydia's heart.

A day after the auction of his grandparent's farm, Joel strode with purpose toward the farmhouse-turned-business. He had a wrong to make right. A bell jingled above Joel Yoder's head as he entered Lydia's Amish Shoppe through the front door. Newspapers and bubble wrap littered the floor. Boxes were stacked high in every corner.

He and the shopkeeper had one thing in common—boxes packed with nowhere to go.

The realtor had neglected to inform Joel the house was being used as a business, a ploy which had to be in favor of the *Englisch* buyer, who paid handsomely after all. Had Joel known, he would have . . . what? Truth be told, he had no idea. But he never would have been so unfair to the Amish business woman who rented the place. Would she believe he was ignorant of her existence? Even though he lived all the way in Ontario, she could reasonably expect him to have known the details about his rental property. She couldn't know his realtor had left him under the impression both the land and the building were rented by her brother. Easy enough, since he never would have guessed a single, Amish woman had turned the old house into a shop—a profitable success, to boot.

All night, he'd tossed and turned. The woman who drove up the price of sale haunted his sleep.

She'd done him a favor. He'd put her out of business.

More regret.

Now, she sat perched on a countertop beside a rustic cash register. Strands of golden-brown hair fell loose from her prayer *kapp* to frame her heart-shaped face and delicate chin. Green eyes held his gaze moments before averting under thick lashes.

She swiped the back of her hand at the moisture on her cheeks. He hadn't meant to intrude. Didn't she hear the bell when he came in?

"*Vass is letz?*" What's wrong? His question made him sound even more out of touch than he'd already proved himself to be. Joel twisted his hat in his hands. He was no expert on women, but even he could surmise the answer. If only he'd done so sooner.

"I'll be fine. *Danki.*" She jumped down and smoothed her hands along the front of her apron. She stood tall, a few inches shy of his six feet. "How may I help you?"

No more tears. The sight of her so brokenhearted pained him. He'd come to Lancaster to sell his inheritance, not ruin another woman's life.

"I'm Joel," he offered, but her expression told him she already knew who he was. Since his arrival in Millers Creek, everyone knew who he was before he could offer an introduction. He understood. Word would travel just as fast back home in Ontario. Whenever he could finally arrange his move to Prince Edward Island, their fledgling Amish community would be no different. "And you are Lydia."

She nodded and continued to stare down at her laced fingers. Of course, he hadn't expected an exuberant welcome.

Joel searched for something to say next. "I spoke with your brother, Ben, about the fields. He said you would be here." Her brother had done an admirable job of farming the land Joel rented to him. At least Joel had managed to ensure Ben's arrangement remained in the sale contract.

More silence.

Joel cleared his throat. "I'll be here until the final closing in two weeks. I can help you." Nervousness loosened his tongue, and guilt prodded him to offer more. "I can pack or do heavy lifting."

Her lips twitched against an almost smile at the extended olive branch. At least he hoped, until he followed Lydia's line of vision to his hat tapping against his thigh. Stupid, nervous habit. He forced his hand to still.

Maybe he should stick to his original intent. "This was once my grandmother's house. I'd like to look around, if it's not too much trouble."

"No trouble at all." She turned and resumed packing with a relieved sigh.

Had he ever met this woman? His last visit had been so long ago; but for sure, he'd remember her if he'd seen her before. He wasn't likely to ever forget such a pretty face. He would have noticed her at the auction, even if she hadn't been the only woman bidding. He had to wonder if she'd always had as much gumption as she showed yesterday. An Amish woman like Lydia Miller would have made an impression on him, no matter their ages.

"Would you like me to show you around?" Lydia interrupted his thoughts. Her cheeks were a pretty pink.

He hadn't intended to remain standing so close. What in the world? He'd been staring at her. He cleared his throat. "It has been a long time, and much has changed."

"For the best, I hope." She moved away from him. Her long fingers slid across the wood grain above her head. Her movements were graceful and accentuated her slender features. "You can see the original cabinetry has been preserved."

Joel better focus more on the architecture and less on Lydia. In fact, he did recognize a resemblance to his own childhood home in Ontario. The place resurrected a sense of connection to his *datt*. After his father's death and mother's remarriage, the house had been sold. Joel had been five years old. What memories he had, he held dear.

"Yes, it looks very similar to my grandfather's work at home. In Canada, I mean, in the house he built there before my father was born. I think he built this one a short time before moving to Canada at the start of the Second World War." Clearly his grandfather always planned to return here, since he'd never sold the place. But decades later, when the time came to return, Joel's *datt* was already in love with his *mamm*. They married and remained in Ontario. His father's dreams encompassed far more than time granted him, when his life was cut short in a farming accident. Above all, Joel desired to see those dreams realized. Now, everything seemed to be coming to pass without Joel.

Lydia stepped out into the larger part of the room. "When we removed the walls, my brother built custom pillars to match. I wanted to maintain the heritage of the house as much as possible, even though the space needed to be open for the shop." She turned to face him. "I was truly grateful for your permission to make the changes. I hope you are pleased."

Permission? Joel never knew about the shop, much less structural changes. When the realtor was forced to explain Lydia's circumstance, he acted as though Lydia's business was of no consequence.

Joel's jaw clenched at the injustice. "I was never informed."

Color drained from Lydia's face. Her fingers fussed with the stray hairs on her face. "Your realtor s-s-spoke as if we increased the value for you."

Joel tried to relax the muscle tightening his jaw. His frustration was misleading the poor woman. "If I had known, I would have consented. No one did me more favors than you, when it comes to the value of the property at auction." An image of her in a price war against the bidder in cahoots with the realtor flashed through his thoughts, as it had a million times the night before. "You've made a fine shop."

"*Danki.*" An unconvinced thank you, if ever he heard one. She tucked her chin to hide her face.

Her modesty drew him to her, making him wish he could convince her all she had done was an impressive accomplishment. He held back. The praise would likely make her uncomfortable.

The sound of the front door bell announced someone's arrival in the store. A teenage girl sprinted toward Lydia, skidding to a stop when her head turned in Joel's direction. Her mouth dropped open as if she were about to speak, but she remained mute. Her blonde hair had come loose from her *kapp.* In fact, she was one of the most disheveled Amish girls Joel had ever seen. Her rounded eyes suggested Joel appeared to be more monster than man. Joel smiled to reassure her. Instead of relaxing, she emitted a perfect croak as her gaping mouth finally closed. With a great deal of effort, Joel held back the laughter threatening to burst from his lips.

The same amusement bubbled out of Lydia, who failed to contain her laugh. She wrapped an arm around the girl's shoulders. "Anna is a little shy. Can you give us a minute?"

More than happy to oblige, he roamed around to admire Lydia's craftsmanship. Bolts of fabric for quilts and clothing stood in straight lines against a back wall. Drawers labeled in calligraphy were stocked with sewing supplies. Near the large front window, simple hand-crafted chairs and bookracks formed a semi-circle around a woven rug like an invitation to sit for a spell. He sat and stretched his legs straight out in front of himself.

Someday, a shop like this would be a perfect addition in New Hope. The Prince Edward Island Amish community had only just begun in March. His brother and sister-in-law, Abe and Sarah, were the first Amish to settle on the island. A picture of their buggy traveling down an island roadway even made headlines in the Canadian papers. Abe and Sarah weren't alone for long. Five other families had followed close behind them. And Joel planned to be the next. All had been right on schedule until Rachel had bailed on him.

Joel leaned forward and held his aching head in his hands. New Hope? Not for him, apparently.

"Where will you stay?" Lydia asked from behind him.

Joel lifted his head up to see her walk around to face him. "I've been staying at a motel." And the cab fares were getting expensive.

"Anna was sent by her *mamm* to offer for you to stay with the Stoltzfus family." Lydia nodded toward the back door, where Anna stood waiting in silence.

"It's a kind offer. Anna might not survive my presence for two whole weeks." The truth was Joel didn't know whether he wanted to spend that long with total strangers himself, even though they were Amish.

Lydia summed him up with a sympathetic nod. "The attic room here still has a bed."

"How much?"

"What?"

"How much do you charge? If you beat the motel, I'll take it. Plus, the cab fees are killing me. Yoders are thrifty, you know." He'd spoken before thinking. Guilt for all he owed this woman was driving him to offer money to stay in a place he still owned—for two more weeks, anyway. She had to think he was *farukt*.

She laughed. Apparently, she'd decided he was joking instead of crazy. Joel reveled in her genuine amusement—far more welcome than tears, even if he was the joke. "We've been known to sleep in our buggies to save from paying for a hotel."

Another laugh.

Ya. He liked the sound.

"I'll tell Anna to let Miriam know you will be staying here. You are welcome to come to my brother's house for meals, if it suits you. His house is across the street. He rents your fields. But you know that, of course." Lydia's last words trailed behind her as she walked toward Anna, who now held onto the door handle as if her life depended on a fast escape.

Looking for a way to be useful, Joel picked up a broom. He couldn't lounge in a chair when he owed this woman such an enormous debt. Not only did he owe her gratitude, but also some sort of recompense for her livelihood. She had a shop with no home. He would soon have a farm but no wife. He knew too well the pain of losing all of one's hard work and years of effort.

When his engagement to Rachel ended, Joel appealed for an exception to the rule allowing only married men and families to join the new community for the first few years. Bishop Nafziger wouldn't change his mind, not even for his step-son.

No wife. No deal.

"Did you say something?" Lydia had returned and her right brow was quirked upward.

"*Nay.*" Had he? He hoped his thoughts were not so transparent.

"If I work hard enough this morning, do you think you might show me around Millers Creek during a break for lunch?"

Her right brow arched a little higher. "*Fleeya.*"

Maybe? What kind of answer was that? "I'll buy lunch at the bakery down the road."

The question in her eyes turned cheeky. "Well, then, I can't miss an opportunity to see a Yoder on a spending spree."

The sound of his own laughter was the best surprise of the day. Lydia Miller might be the exact medicine he needed after the stress of the past month.

A warning rang in Joel's conscience to proceed with caution. His courtship notions had recently landed him in a heap of trouble. His heart was supposed to be broken—not galloping away like an untethered stallion.

CHAPTER TWO

Two weeks had passed since Joel Yoder blew into Millers Creek like a whirlwind to turn Lydia's life upside down. Lydia stretched her arm across the doorway to reach the doorknob and close up shop. Through the screen door, she saw Joel turn and wave as he strolled down the lane away from the shop. She returned his see-you-later nod and shut the door.

"Oh goodness, Lydia. I thought the man would never leave." Anna poked her head around the doorframe of the workroom where she'd hidden.

"He won't bite you, Anna. After all the days and hours he's spent helping around here, you should know better by now. You could give yourself a chance to like him. How else will you ever make new friends?"

"Well, I just want things back to how they were around here." The teen crossed her arms.

"He's been very kind." More than necessary, but Lydia wasn't about to fuel Anna's tendency toward romantic notions. Fantastical notions. Nothing Anna would ever actually put into action for herself. Ach, but the girl was a dreamer. "What's done is done."

"Humph, well at least I found something interesting." Anna had a sly grin and held a hand behind her back.

"Like what?"

"Like valuable information on the Canadian interloper."

"Careful. Keep talking that way, and your *mamm* will confiscate those spy novels again. Joel Yoder is not an interloper. Do you even know what the word means?"

"What I know is this land should belong to our people. I can't stand to see the Yoder place turned over to an *Englischer*."

"Truly, Anna, we should show love no matter if our neighbor is Amish or *Englisch*."

A small lump formed in Lydia's throat. She may not approve of Anna's attitude but was hard-pressed not to share the disappointment. The Yoder fields of mown hay and grazing Holstein dairy cows were the gateway to Millers Creek. Lydia couldn't imagine the community any way other than she'd known all her life. A new subdivision with houses squeezed in tight rows was not an option she preferred either. Yet she knew in a time past, things had been different.

Herman Yoder, Joel's grandfather, moved with his new bride to Canada during the Second World War. Eventually, he returned with his wife and daughters to re-settle in Millers Creek. But his son, Joel's father, had married a Canadian and remained behind. When Joel's father died, everyone supposed Joel's grandmother held onto the home in the hope her grandson would return to continue the family line in Lancaster. Clearly, Joel had no such desire. And why shouldn't he be free to pursue his purpose elsewhere, so long as it pleased *Gott*?

Anna waved the yellowed paper in front of Lydia. "Not even a bit interested?"

"You're up to no good. Let me see."

Anna stepped out of reach. "I'd rather read it to you."

How much harm could reading an old piece of paper do? "Fine."

The brittle paper crinkled as Anna smoothed it out on the countertop; then after a dramatic intake of breath, Anna read aloud.

Gott will make a path for your dreams to begin a new settlement for the people. Choose your wife wisely . . .

"Stop!" Was Anna reading a private letter? "What have you done?" Lydia laid her hand on top of the paper, as if to protect the contents.

Questions swirled in Lydia's head until she felt dizzy. "Where did you get this?"

"I found it in a drawer of the old writing desk you asked me to dust." Anna's head dropped down. She continued in a repentant tone, "I didn't intend to snoop. I was just bored. Everything has been dusted and cleaned a hundred times already. I shouldn't have read it."

"*Nay*, Anna, you shouldn't have." Lydia could see through her splayed fingers the clear address to Joel. She wondered how long ago his grandmother penned the words to him.

Anna let go of the letter. "Why doesn't he have a wife?"

Beulah Yoder had passed nearly seven years ago. But then, if Joel was close in age to Lydia's thirty years, he would have been more than old enough to be thinking on marriage prior to his grandmother's death. Lydia stuffed the page back into the envelope, then deep into her apron pocket for safe-keeping.

"I wouldn't know. And don't be imagining things. You've done enough."

The matter was the man's own affair. He could have his reasons for remaining unmarried. Lydia did.

"Maybe you'll find out tonight, when you have your talk." Anna stretched out the last word with a teasing reference to Joel's request to speak with her after supper.

"Maybe it's time for you to go home." Lydia shooed at her with a wave, then put on her best school teacher voice. "And take your mischievous ways with you."

Despite her antics, Lydia loved Anna like a sister. If her youngest sister had lived, she might have been the joy to Lydia's heart that Anna had become.

"I overheard *Datt* telling *Mamm* that Joel was desperate for a wife. Up there in Canada, the bishop . . . "

"Hush, Anna. I don't want to hear any gossip." Besides, she'd already heard all the rumors about Joel's step-father, the bishop. *He encourages Bible study. He teaches Scripture has greater authority than the Ordnung.* On and on, the list continued about the progressive bishop. Lydia pointed to a full trash bag. "Take that with you, please. I need to finish here and go help prepare supper."

Why did she care whom Joel married? The world would be a happier place if everyone would mind their own business. And Joel Yoder's matrimonial affairs were none of hers.

Lydia locked the front door behind Anna and scanned the room from left to right as she turned. The solitary evidence of six years of business manifested as a mere bucket with a protruding mop handle. She tip-toed in socked feet across the dry floor to retrieve the bucket and headed out the back way.

A chill wind reminded her not to forget her shawl. In a hurry to toss the dirty water into the bushes, Lydia propelled the bucket forward when the sight of Hiram's buggy stopped her short.

Wetness slapped her dress against her legs, and cold water soaked her socks. Whether the subsequent shivers came from the drenching or the vision of Hiram Glick, she couldn't tell.

Ach, to be able to hide like Anna.

But there was no escape.

Hiram's legs weren't exceptionally long, but he moved them quickly. He stood a couple inches shorter than Lydia—not an uncommon occurrence as she was taller than many men. However, with Hiram, the difference was pronounced as he always pressed himself right into her personal space.

Lydia took a preemptive step backward before he reached her.

She'd avoided the man ever since the auction. Yet she'd suspected he would pursue his cause. The reason she'd given for not wanting to court him had been an unwillingness to give up her business should she marry. The excuse wasn't a lie, just not the whole truth. Besides, his own brother was the no-brainer part of her this-will-never-work equation. Why he wanted Lydia after her history with Simeon was the real mystery. He had to be a little off in the head.

How had life come to this?

Hiram's thick hair and long, angular nose reminded her enough of Simeon to make her step away from his rapid approach.

"It's not natural." Hiram was talking without any context other than the one in Lydia's mind. She had to agree with him this once. His obsession with marrying her felt very unnatural.

"I won't change my mind, Hiram."

"You can't still be pining over my brother. He's got his own family now. His wife comes from sturdy stock. Ain't likely he'll be a widower any day soon."

Lydia choked on a harsh laugh. Hiram's chickens weren't laying regular, for sure. She didn't want his brother, Simeon, nor his wounds of deceit.

"It's not a funny thing, Lydia. A woman should marry and have children. Are you *farukt?*"

Crazy, no. Lonely, yes. But loneliness beat the idea of company with this obtuse man day after day.

Once again Lydia was reminded of how she could never be like other Amish women. She didn't deserve to be a mother. Her past held the proof. If she told Hiram the truth, he'd leave her alone. But Hiram Glick was the last man on earth to whom she would lay bare her soul.

"I have to get my things and be on my way. Let's not talk about this now." Clinging to her unhooked shawl, Lydia fled across the street to her brother's house. She needed a hot shower to wash away more than filthy mop water. What she really needed was a new life.

Was there a place where an Amish woman like Lydia could be accepted? Joel talked incessantly about the new church community on Prince Edward Island. According to him, New Hope was an Amish utopia, which definitely excluded Lydia. Even Joel couldn't join without a wife. The bishop wouldn't allow it. Too bad a husband and wife couldn't be just friends. Heaven knew, no Amish man would agree to such a thing.

Joel was grateful for the familiarity of an Amish home and the hospitality of Lydia's brother. Ever since his arrival, the family had accepted him in a show of benevolence he was sure he didn't deserve. After spending his day with a realtor and buyer, whose words and actions were filled with contradictions, the Miller children's innocent chatter throughout the meal was welcome diversion.

Ben and his wife, Mary, sat at opposite ends of the table. Lydia sat tall and straight across from Joel. Not a hair out of place. He'd rarely seen her without loose strands of hair falling from under her *kapp*. Her hard work these past two weeks served him up a plentiful helping of guilt.

Her hair and clothes were in order more than usual, but she appeared distracted. Despite his attempts to get her attention, she kept her eyes averted. She swept up her plate along with the others from the table, as if concealing how little she ate.

Was the next day's closing on the farmhouse the source of her distress, or was he? If she had an idea of the offer he was about to make, she'd shown no sign. In fact, he'd tried to gauge her possible response with hints, but she never seemed to understand. She had agreed to a walk with him after supper as more of a time for a chat between friends, rather than the important business Joel had in mind. If only he had more time . . . but he had to leave soon. He had no choice but to present his proposition this evening.

Ben interrupted Joel's thoughts. "Will you join me for a game of checkers?"

Joel had spent all afternoon rehearsing what he needed to say to Lydia. Too bad he'd not considered how to deflect Ben from anticipating another evening of checkers.

"Lydia promised me a walk. As much as I like to spend an evening around a game, the company of a *goot* woman can't be beat."

Lydia's cheeks pinked as he'd noticed anytime she was the center of attention. By her boldness at the auction, he wouldn't have pegged her to be bashful.

Mary spoke up. "When you get back, we can have some pie and a cup of *kaffi.*"

Ben shrugged as though evening strolls with men were commonplace for Lydia. The thought surprised Joel with unexpected disappointment. Somehow, he'd assumed she didn't have a beau. He may be about to make a bigger idiot of himself than he was already prepared to do.

"Don't take too long. I can't promise how much pie will be left." Ben laid a hand on Lydia's shoulder and gave her an approving look as he left the room. Then again, maybe Ben guessed more about the business at hand than he was letting on.

How could he? No real courting had taken place over the last two weeks. He and Lydia had worked themselves to the bone. He hadn't had time for romance or wooing. What they did develop was a terrific working relationship. They made an excellent team. She'd said as much herself.

"Shall we go?" Joel asked Lydia.

"*Ya.* I'll need to get my shawl."

The sage color of her dress made the green of her eyes darker. When she reached to retrieve a crocheted shawl from a peg by the door, he noticed her feminine figure. How could a man not take note? But she wasn't his to look upon with such thoughts. And Joel knew she might not ever be, even as much as he had prayed for *Gott* to make a way.

Joel cleared his throat. Careful not to touch her, he reached behind her head to take his hat from the same row of pegs. She looked up, and the space between them shrank to a mere breath apart.

The wall stopped her attempt to step backward, so Joel pushed the door open to give her room. Her arm brushed against his. How did an innocent touch take his breath as sure as a well-intended kiss?

Trailing a few feet behind, he shook off the sensation before step-
ping into a rhythm beside her. "I thought we might walk to the pond."

"Sure." She side-stepped and widened the gap between them.

Joel was under no illusion of Lydia holding an interest in him
beyond friendship or business. Over the past days, he'd begun to feel
a great deal more. He didn't expect the same from her in such a short
time. He just wished she wasn't quite as clear about her aversion to
him as more than a friend.

Pride was a sin, but to feel a fool in front of a beautiful woman
was a humbling Joel did not relish. Yet an apology to Lydia was the
proper place to start and long over-due.

"There's an *Englischer* in Prince Edward Island who has worked
closely with our congregation in finding land to purchase. I learned
to trust him, as did the bishop and elders. However, I may have grown
careless when it came to finding such a man to help me with the
handling of my property here."

A sincere apology didn't need a preamble. He had to get to the
point. "I never knew about the Amish Shoppe or about you, Lydia. If
I had known, I would have done things differently. I am very sorry."

Lydia stopped walking and faced him. She held her hands together,
but he could see the small tremor she tried to hide. "If you need forgiveness, I'll gladly give it. But in my eyes, you're not to blame."

Ya, he was. She'd already forgiven him like a faithful Amish woman
should do. He'd known as much by her actions. He still owed her more.
How different his life may have been if he'd met Lydia years earlier—
before he gave into the pressure to court Rachel.

If only Lydia had someone to help her absorb the shock of a loss of
income. She was alone, except for Ben and his family. She was young

and too ambitious to live off the charity of the people. They would expect her to marry.

Joel had a feeling she valued her independence over marriage. The painstaking care she had taken to create such a charming shop indicated she planned to support herself for a long while. Joel wanted better answers for her, but all he had was the plain truth to tell her.

The small footpath through the trees behind Ben's house soon widened into an open field where a pond lay at the bottom of the slope. He'd come here to pray each day at sunrise since he had discovered the spot and a wooden bench at the tree line.

He reached out with the lightest touch of his fingers to her elbow. "*Kumm*, Lydia. Let's go where we can sit. I need to ask you another question."

She faced him with her right brow quirked high in question. "And I have to be seated to hear it?"

Her teasing eased his dread. As long as it didn't change to outright hilarity when she heard his offer. He looked across the water and prayed for the right words.

"Well, I'm seated." She looked up at him with a teasing grin.

Joel inhaled deeply and sat beside her. He'd begin with the option she was sure to find the most satisfactory. The prices in Lancaster were dear, but a clear conscience was worth more.

"I've found a small lot for sale. It's large enough to build a new shop and still within a bike's ride from here."

"I appreciate your effort, but there's little chance I can afford it." She looked down at her hands in her lap.

He knew all the money from her years as a schoolteacher had been invested into the renovations. The knowledge only heightened his guilt. "I mean to buy it for you."

She swung her head up to stare straight at him. Her eyes held suspicion and warning. Had he offended her?

His break-up with Rachel raced through his mind. He'd hurt her by putting his own dreams and ambition above hers. This time, he tried to get his priorities in the right order.

Could he explain without dragging the embarrassment of his broken engagement into the mix? "I don't want to leave you here like this." If he was telling the whole truth, he didn't want to leave her at all. If he was telling the whole truth, he'd tell her about Rachel.

Her glare softened, and her eyes misted before she looked down again.

"Not an option, Joel. I am fully aware you cannot purchase your farm on Prince Edward Island with the difference."

If only he could deny her reason and give her what she wanted. He couldn't lie. All he had left to offer was the one solution he scarcely dared hope she would accept.

Dear Gott, show me the way to ask what I must. Joel drew a deep breath in preparation for his next offer, but Lydia spoke first.

"Your grandmother intended for your inheritance to fulfill your *Gott*-given purpose. I won't snatch it away for my own dreams."

"How can you know that?" If she'd thrown a cold glass of water in his face, Joel couldn't have been more surprised.

How well had Lydia known his grandmother before she died? She'd been gone for seven years. Before she died, *Gammi* wrote often. She believed his *datt's* vision for a new church was worth all the planning and waiting. And praying. *Gammi* believed in the power of prayer.

Lydia squirmed on the bench, suddenly a little too small for comfort. "I think you better tell me the other idea."

To love as Gott loves is always the right choice. Joel's heart echoed back the advice penned in every letter to him until his grandmother's death. Could he love Lydia the way she deserved?

There must be a better way to make his plea than in such a confounded hurry. But a farm on the island was waiting for his signature for purchase. And so much work had to be done before spring. If Joel lost this opportunity, the next could be years in the making.

Lydia was right. *Gammi* had understood both his dream and his father's. She knew the importance of a new church community in an area where farmers could prosper and the ways of the people could be passed to future generations. First his father, and now Joel envisioned a place where Amish men and women could grow in the Lord together, where personal Bible study was as important as adherence to the *Ordnung*, where hearts and lives were healed by love and faith. If anyone ever needed such a place, Lydia did. She tried to hide her hurt, but Joel knew she carried some deep burdens.

"Lydia?" His tongue caught on the roof of his mouth, as dry as a sun-parched creek bed in August.

A renegade wisp of hair wafted free about her face. Her hair so often flying free from her *kapp* matched her spirit, independent with a mind of its own.

She was beautiful, loyal, and hard-working. He believed his final idea would serve them both well. He ought to tell her about Rachel first. Shame weighed down his tongue like lead.

"*Ya?*" She was waiting. Her eyes searched his face for the truth. "I'm right here."

Joel cleared his throat and tried again. "You could marry me."

CHAPTER THREE

Lydia couldn't think straight sitting so close to Joel. She walked over to a large oak and leaned against the powerful trunk for strength. The rough bark scratched her back.

Why couldn't she answer? *Nay, Joel. Danki all the same.*

How hard could that be?

She'd managed to ward off Hiram for another day. Joel would be gone soon enough. Surely, she could manage to reject him for a day or so.

Ach. Men.

She'd spent the past decade shunning thoughts of romance and marriage. Yet somehow, she still wanted a proposal to amount to more than a handshake on a deal.

Why then was giving an answer so difficult? To have known him for only a fortnight was reason enough to refuse his unexpected offer, but she wasn't a naïve young *maydel*.

Joel was unlike most men. She'd grown to trust her own judgment on a man's character. A lesson learned the hard way. No matter how honorable and deserving Joel may be, the fact remained she was not.

Joel's comforting, clean, citrus scent gave away his presence behind her. He didn't frighten her. Some men did, but not Joel. She turned her head to see him prop his shoulder against the side of the tree opposite her.

"Lydia?"

His thoughts likely echoed her own. What was she to say to him? Joel was the kind of man she never wanted to hurt. "I cannot give you an answer yet." He twisted his hat through his fingers, and the lump in her throat plummeted to her stomach. How could she explain? "I'm just not ready . . . for that."

Tomorrow was the closing, and he'd be gone. Her chest ached at the thought, but his departure was for the best. She'd manage to skirt the question for a day somehow—as long as he didn't know how badly she wanted to run from here.

He moved closer and spoke in a hushed tone. "You could go on as you do now. An Amish shop would be a terrific business on the island. I'd build it right away. I don't want to change you, Lydia. I admire what you've done."

She could lose herself in those eyes of his. Lost in an imaginary world where she was cherished and honored. What would it be like to stay there forever? *Ach*, she was as silly as Anna.

"The house I plan to purchase is large enough for you to get away from me anytime you like." Joel's voice returned to the banter she enjoyed from him.

"You're very funny."

He touched her shoulder, and she felt the same shock of warmth as when she'd accidentally brushed against him earlier.

She dared not be swayed by physical attraction. Marriage was a blessing not meant for her. Her eyes squeezed shut against the memory of the accident which took her young sister's life. *Nay*, Lydia was not fit for motherhood. Why did Joel bother himself over her future? She'd never made any attempt to obligate him. "You worry too much over me."

"Do I?"

"I'm not as fragile as you fear." She'd weather this storm somehow.

"I'd never accuse you of being weak. Does that mean I'm not allowed to care what happens to you?"

He pricked her heart. Her family cared. As did Miriam Stoltzfus in her own way, despite how she got under Lydia's skin. But Joel's words fanned a warmth down to her soul. An understanding man like Joel Yoder was a rare treasure. A day of resisting the pull to flee with him may prove too great a temptation.

"Thank you for being a friend to me." She looked up long enough to see the left corner of his lips turn upward. What a comfort his smile had provided over the past two weeks.

She knew for certain letting go of their friendship would be painful. But marriage? She spun around to hide her nearness to surrender.

Joel blew out a breath. "I'm on your side, Lydia. I want to see you happy. We can begin as friends. I'd never ask for anything you aren't willing to give. The island is a place for a new beginning for us both. A new start. A chance for faith and hope to grow."

Her own shop in a community where no one knew anything about her was too incredible an offer to ignore. What did Miriam say about *Gott* and overcoming the past? She'd been serving penance for her mistakes for fourteen years. Could New Hope offer her a clean slate?

A soft current of air brushed the exposed skin on the back of her neck and soothed her spirit like a caress from Heaven. She had to try. Her future in Millers Creek offered nothing.

Would Joel still want her, even if she couldn't be a real wife to him? A fresh start was one thing. Trusting herself with a child was another.

She turned to answer, but the broad, tall figure she sought was disappearing down the path where the sun dipped out of sight.

Joel's whole body ached as he forced himself away from Lydia. The determination to leave her unpressured while making her decision required more power than he'd known himself to possess. Yet for both their sakes, she needed to choose without any more stress than the situation already heaped upon her.

Had he truly offered to relinquish all his marital privileges to a woman who drew him like Samson to the forbidden honeycomb? He rammed his hat back onto his harebrained head and vowed his lips sealed before he uttered any further insanity.

He aimed his path toward the privacy of the empty farmhouse across the street and almost ran into a shadowy figure of a man who stepped into his way. The short, hawkish Amish man moved closer.

"I'm looking for Lydia." His eyes pierced Joel with unspoken accusations, and then he sniffed a punctuation of disapproval.

Unwilling to share Lydia's whereabouts with a man he didn't know, Joel nodded toward Ben's place. "You might try asking her brother."

"The bishop is there waiting to see her." His head bobbed up and down as he stretched on his toes to look over Joel's shoulders.

"I'm not hiding her behind my back." Joel looked down at the man, who stood uncomfortably close. Joel ignored the inclination to step backward, in case the man might try to get around him. He didn't want him anywhere near Lydia. Why in the world had he left her alone near dark? "I expect she will return home soon enough. Why not wait?"

The man's chest puffed outward and raised his frame a little higher. "The bishop—"

"—has the good sense to wait at the house. *Ya?*" Joel leveled the man with the best son-of-a-bishop stare-down he could muster.

The man spun around and headed toward the Millers' house. Only after his wiry frame stepped out of sight did Joel turn around to go find Lydia.

A few yards away, she snuck out from behind a tree to meet him. His protective instincts reached to pull her close. To his surprise, she didn't back away; instead, a sadness in the depths of her green eyes beckoned his comfort.

"Lydia?"

"Will you come with me?" She shivered.

She heard. No wonder—the man squawked as noisily as a threatened cockerel. Joel reached for her hand. Her long, slender fingers slid with a warm and perfect fit into his outstretched palm.

She looked down at their hands and bit her lip before speaking. "The bishop will have come to encourage me to marry. And Hiram will say I no longer have any excuse to deny his proposal."

"That crowing bird-face's name is Hiram? You would marry him?"

She jerked her hand to get free, but Joel refused to let go.

"I will not!" Determination replaced her sadness. She tugged again.

"*Goot.*" Joel pulled back with a gentle squeeze. He smiled, and her hand relaxed in his again.

She stood a breath apart without any hint of shyness. "Joel, I understand the desperation of feeling your future slip away. But is it reason enough to marry me—a stranger?"

The question was fair. He'd spent long nights in search of the answer. He'd known Lydia for only a couple weeks. He'd known Rachel for two decades. Why did his heart say yes to the one and no to the other?

"We're friends. That's the foundation of a happy marriage." He'd believed so when he thought he'd marry Rachel. But now? Oh, he wanted so much more. Rachel had been right. She deserved someone who really loved her. So did Lydia. And for the first time in his life, Joel felt he'd found a woman with whom he could fall deeply in love. They just needed more time, which wasn't a luxury either could afford at the moment.

Her eyes pled for honesty. "And if that is all we ever have? Because I am not ready for more, Joel. I may never be."

"I will never regret our friendship, Lydia." His conscience warned he was tripping over the dangerous precipice of a lie. He knew he would always want more. Instinct told him she'd run if he admitted he could be falling in love with her already. He'd be slow and gentle with her until he could show her how he felt.

He didn't believe this would end unhappily. Love would grow. He would do all in his power to win her heart. He took her other hand in his and held both close to his heart. "I promised not to ask for more than you are willing to give. A promise I'll keep, Lydia."

She stood so close. If only a kiss wouldn't be breaking the promise he just made.

"Well, then, I will marry you, Joel Yoder." She stepped to his side with her shoulders back and her head up.

Side by side. Not hand in hand, yet, but together. A delight in the rightness of the moment settled deep into his heart. *Samen vit, samen thuis.* The old way of saying, "We're in this together," literally meant "leaving together, going home together." As friends was enough. For now.

They strode toward the three men waiting on her brother's porch. Joel paused halfway across the yard. "Would you like to go in the back door? I can talk to the men outside."

"*Nay*, I'll go with you." A laugh bubbled out of her.

"I didn't think you'd want to miss the look on bird-beak's face."

"That's not nice." Lydia's full laugh contradicted her admonishment.

Joel took heart from Lydia's change of mood, until he imagined the looks on a few other faces when he arrived home with a new bride. He hadn't even mentioned Rachel to Lydia. How would he explain now? Was the fact he'd been engaged to Rachel even important anymore?

Wedding season was in full swing among the churches, now that the harvest was complete. He and Lydia could be husband and wife in under a fortnight. His *mamm* and step-*datt*, Bishop Nafziger, would be surprised, but even more thankful he finally married. His half-brother, Abe, would be relieved Joel was joining him after all. His sister-in-law, Sarah . . . Well, she'd come around eventually. Abe and Sarah would be welcoming their first child to the family in the spring. Joel had a lot of courting to do to with his soon-to-be wife to catch up with his little brother in filling his home with children.

But if *Gott* was willing . . .

CHAPTER FOUR

"Come in." Lydia answered the gentle rap on her bedroom door as she stood by the bed in her wedding dress.

"It is I, Salome." Joel's *mamm* peeked around the door. She was a small woman with gray hair pulled under her *kapp*, which was more conical than the heart-like shape of the Lancaster covering. Clearly, Joel's height had not come from his *mamm*; but her dark brown eyes, which sparkled in the light, were the same as his.

Salome stepped further into the room and pushed the door closed behind her. "Your dress is very nice."

"You don't mind the color?" Lydia looked down at the forest green she'd chosen rather than the traditional royal blue of most girls in her church. There would likely be whispers, but Lydia didn't care anymore. Soon, she'd be gone, and the disapproval couldn't reach her.

"Why would I? Today is your wedding day, and green suits you well." Salome offered her a sweet smile. "I believe Joel will be pleased." She was soft-spoken with a calm surety that put Lydia at ease. Salome was right about Joel. For some reason, he took special notice when she dressed in green. This shade was a deeper hue than any of her others, making it both different and formal for such a sacred occasion.

Sacred.

Lydia pressed her clammy palms together.

Salome sat on the bed and patted the mattress as if for Lydia to have a seat.

As Lydia settled beside her, Joel's *mamm* took her hand and cupped it between her own. A lump swelled in Lydia's throat. For years, she'd hardly known the touch of another. Then Joel had taken her hands, and now his mother did the same. Oh, her nieces and nephews climbed into her lap when they were small, and their affection was precious. This was different. Salome Nafziger, a woman she barely knew, sparked a tender assurance of her care through a simple touch. Joining this family was going to be very different, for sure.

"I wanted to wish you well. Samuel and I are very pleased Joel has found a wife from among his father's people here in Lancaster."

"*Danki.*" Lydia thought of how kind Joel's grandmother, Beulah Yoder, had always been to her. Would she be pleased? All night, she'd wrestled with doubts. Salome didn't know much about Lydia. Beulah had seen everything.

"I do not wish to intrude for long. I . . . I know you must miss your *mamm* today." Salome bowed her head.

The rare mention of her mother surprised Lydia. What was she to say? They never spoke of the departed. And yet, Salome's recognition of her *mamm* on this day comforted her heart like her *mamm's* smile used to do.

"Our church district is less strict, as I am sure Joel has explained." She paused as if she must choose her words carefully. "You have so many changes ahead of you. I hope you will feel safe to come to me for help."

Joel hadn't inherited his *mamm's* short stature, but he had her tender ways. "*Danki.* I will try."

"In time, everything will work out fine." Salome stood to leave. "Someday, we will talk more. I won't be at New Hope for a couple months, since I will be helping my daughter in Ontario with her new *bobli*. When I return, we will get to know each other. You may be surprised how much we have in common."

Surprised? Lydia would be astounded to find she had anything in common with Salome Nafziger. They were even different in their Amish traditions. She wondered that her own bishop hadn't made a fuss over the issue. Was he so relieved to be rid of her, he'd overlooked the more liberal views of Joel's church? Well, she wasn't about to ask him.

She'd only just met Samuel Nafziger, Joel's step-father, who would be her new bishop. He struck her as a man of God to whom she could ask a question. Such a thing would be a change, for sure.

As the church service neared an end, Lydia's pulse quickened. At the conclusion of the sermon, she and Joel would make their marriage vows before everyone. Especially, *Gott*.

A tremble traveled up her spine.

She felt Joel's eyes on her, as she had often during the past hour. If he was experiencing any nervousness, he'd given no sign. She stared at her fingers clasped in a tight twist in her lap. Her thumb began to tremor, and she bit her lower lip. A dam of tears threatened to unleash. Just as she closed her eyes, the warm sensation of Joel's hand over hers steadied her composure.

The relief was welcome, until she remembered the bishop was watching. Then before Joel could receive a reprimand from the minister, he removed his hand from hers to a proper distance beside her. How was he so confident?

She should have told him. The day he asked her to marry him, she should have explained the reason she couldn't be a true wife to him. Ever. How would she explain now? Their peculiar marriage would become even harder. Would he really never expect more from her than friendship? Because friendship was all she had a right to offer.

A harvest moon lit the sky on the evening of their wedding. A kerosene lamp buzzed over a checker game being played by some young people on the porch. Most of the folks left at the house were family. At least, Joel supposed. So many introductions in one day were difficult to remember.

Three weeks after Joel's arrival in Millers Creek, he was a married man. If only by a minor miracle.

Just before the minister called them forward to say their vows, Joel sensed Lydia was close to bolting from the ceremony. He knew the rush into marriage was more difficult for Lydia than for himself. Some women wouldn't make such a drastic move away from family and community, even if they were in love. He hadn't known what to do, other than pray for Lydia to have courage.

He thought back to the day he first saw her. He'd never forget the way she made the *Englisch* bidder sweat. A smile tipped his lips at the memory. *Gott* gave her a courageous spirit, for sure, on that day and this.

His parents had already left for the evening. They were staying at a hotel in Lancaster and leaving early to visit his half-sister, due to have a baby any day in Ontario. A storm system expected to bring the first heavy snow of the season was coming from the west. He and Lydia needed to beat it home, too.

Abe and Sarah hadn't made the trip on such short notice. Abe's not-so-subtle hint had been that Joel was better off without Sarah present. Sarah's disappointment at Joel's quick marriage came as no surprise to Joel. Abe offered assurance his wife would accept Lydia by the time they met. Joel's predictions weren't so positive.

The second wedding meal would soon be served, so Joel headed back into the house.

His bride was busy with the other women.

He leaned against the kitchen doorframe next to Lydia. "Did you make those?" He pointed at the delectable fried pies arranged on the plate in her hand.

"You know so."

"How about hiding a few for us to take with us tomorrow?"

Lydia shrugged. "*Freeyah.*"

"Oh, it's maybe, is it? I've heard that before."

She teased him with a grin. "*Ach,* I already did." She shooed him from the kitchen with a wave of her hand.

Joel turned around to see Amos Stoltzfus, the neighbor with whom Joel had stayed for the past week since closing on the farm. "Best come and eat before all the food gets gone." His eyes shone with merriment.

Joel and Amos sat across the table from a young man who appeared about eighteen or so. His sun-streaked brown hair and strong hands indicated he was used to outdoor labor. "Winston?" Joel believed he recalled the name correctly.

"*Ya.* I'm Amos' nephew." The youth was already digging into his chicken dinner and spoke between mouthfuls. "I was thinking how I wish I was going with you."

"Is that right?"

"Seems to me every state in our country has Amish communities already. Must be an adventure being a part of something new. Being first at a thing. I figure going to Prince Edward Island would be the time of my life."

Joel finished loading his plate from the serving dishes in the center of the table. "It's been a life-long dream of mine, for sure. Land at home in Ontario costs more than ten times as much per acre than on the island. We tried cheaper land in northern Ontario without success for our crops. *Gott* has blessed us with more fertile and affordable land in a beautiful place."

"Maybe I can follow you someday." An eagerness lit Winston's young face.

Amos jabbed Winston with a playful punch. "You'll have to find a wife first. I hear the bishop won't allow an unmarried man to move his church membership to the new settlement for the first few years."

The reminder caused Joel to drop his fork back to his plate. "It's true." He'd always known Amish news spread fast. Had the story made the journey—including the recent break-up with Rachel? Did Lydia already know?

"*Gott* has a way of working out the details." Amos tilted his head toward the women in the other room. Joel followed to see Lydia with a *bobli* perched on her hip. The child cooed and played with the strings dangling from her *kapp*.

Lydia had married him with the clear understanding normal marital privileges were not included. And he had promised to be content. The sight of her with the child wasn't doing him any favors.

"Would have been a terrible misfortune to see her with one of those Glick boys." Amos kept an eye on Joel as he chewed another bite before he continued. "Thought she'd never get over that accident and settle down."

Accident? Joel looked to Lydia, wondering what had been so traumatic for her. Was there more to her stipulations on the marriage than the newness of their relationship? Hiram Glick and who else? Lydia never spoke of another Glick brother. Then again, he'd never told her about Rachel either. How could they begin a marriage with so many secrets?

New Hope members agreed to live transparently before each other and the world around them. They committed to abandon the old ways of shame, which led to secrets and pain. New Hope was meant to be a community built on grace practiced through honesty and forgiveness. Joel's appetite waned. What had he done?

"And I'll tell you who else would be happy with this marriage—your grandmother Yoder. She was fond of Lydia. If she'd been the matchmaking sort, I expect we'd have arrived at this day long ago." The man shook his head. "*Gott's* time is not man's time."

Gammi would approve of Lydia, for sure. Would she be happy with Joel? "She always prayed for *Gott* to direct my path."

"And you believe He has, *nay?*"

"*Ya*, I do." Whether Joel had done everything in order or not, he was certain *Gott* had led him straight to Lydia.

Tomorrow morning, he and Lydia would be traveling the road to Prince Edward Island. Would *Gott* bless this path as *Gammi* had prayed? Surely, the distance was far enough to separate Lydia from whatever pain the past had caused her. Her distress had been evident throughout the service this morning, apparently from more than the usual wedding jitters.

Dear Gott, help us.

CHAPTER FIVE

In less than two days' time, a brisk Pennsylvanian autumn transitioned to a bitter winter on the northerly drive through New England and into Maine.

Were the trip a holiday, Lydia might be able to appreciate the beautiful country zipping past the windows. Instead, her stomach twisted in knotted anticipation of their final destination. Four hours past the Canadian border in New Brunswick, Prince Edward Island was practically on the horizon. The village of Montague, the closest to their rural community, was just a few more hours away.

Eric Peterson, the van driver, called over his shoulder, "Would you like to stop and eat before we cross the bridge over to the island? If I fill up now, we should make it the rest of the way. Those clouds look like they could start dumping snow anytime now, but the temperatures in Charlottetown are above freezing."

Lydia turned to Joel. "There are enough sandwiches left for all of us and a few of Mary's fried pies still. No need to stop at a restaurant, unless . . . " She nodded at Eric.

Joel leaned up toward the driver. "If you're willing to share our simple lunch, then we can stop at a filling station and be on our way ahead of the storm."

The rumble of a belly laugh sounded from the middle-aged driver. "If you're willing to share, I'm more than willing to partake. I might have agreed to drive for nothing but the cost of fuel if I could eat all this good home cookin'. Beats anything I ever got in my trucking days." Eric looked into the rearview mirror at Lydia. "Just don't tell my boss." He laughed at his own joke. "One quick stop, and we'll go over the Federation Bridge to the island. According to the internet, the bridge takes ten minutes to cross by car. It's eight miles long." The man whistled.

A smartphone would intrude on Lydia's simple life in ways she would never trade for the sake of convenience. On this trip, she was thankful for Eric's careful navigation all done so easily on his phone. Not a dull moment had lapsed on the journey. Eric was full of tidbits of information all along the way.

"Lydia?" Joel's voice was quiet. She looked across to him. His brown eyes met hers; then he looked away. "We're almost there." His eyes flitted back to hers. "I hope you will like it."

What made him so uncomfortable all of the sudden? "Is there something you need to tell me?"

"*Ya*, there is something I should have told you, but I cannot explain now." He came as close to her as his seatbelt would allow. She leaned over until their shoulders met. His breath warmed her ear as he whispered, "I want you here with me. No one else but you, Lydia." He pulled back enough for her to see his face. His eyes pled with her for understanding. "Will you remember that when you meet my family?"

What did he mean? They were going to live with his brother and sister-in-law until their home was purchased. Did he foresee a problem? Surely, their differences could not be too great. Abe and Sarah were Amish, after all. Joel told her their own house needed work before they could live in it. She didn't mind. In fact, she looked forward to the renovation.

What was he holding back from her? Lydia held onto her questions for a more private moment.

"I'll try to remember."

Joel rubbed his temples with his forefingers. What else could she say? She had no idea what he was asking of her.

No one else. She'd heard those words before. Nausea surged through her already-upset stomach. *Please, Gott, not Joel, too. Not again.*

Joel's heart squeezed in anticipation. Beyond the hill in front of them, Lydia would get her first glimpse of their future farm. Joel would sign the dotted line of ownership within a week. As soon as they'd unloaded the van, he'd hitched Amazon to Abe's open wagon. He wanted Lydia to have a wide-open view. He'd also managed to procrastinate introducing Lydia to his sister-in-law. Of course, the inevitable was sure to come, as Lydia and Sarah had to live together for a few months, at least.

The weather had changed since he'd been gone. The cold scent of snow from the clouds high above them drifted down into the saltiness of the distant ocean and mixed with the spice of the pines. Long winter grasses blew in the wind of snow's promised arrival.

The cold blew at the kerchief tied over Lydia's *kapp* to protect her ears. Joel held tight to the reins with his left hand while tugging up the collar of his coat with his right. Lydia looked over to him with pity in her eyes.

She unfolded the wool blanket around her shoulders and extended her arm behind his shoulders to cover them both. Joel could have blessed the bitter wind at that moment for bringing her so close. They'd maintained a careful distance since their wedding day. Joel had to if he was going to keep his promise. If only Lydia didn't seem so content to keep him at arm's length.

She pulled her arm back and carefully left a few inches between them, removing the *wunderbaar* warmth of her closeness. Her mouth was set in a straight line, and her jaw clenched.

She'd withdrawn even further from him since the crossing to the island that morning. Was she sorry she married him after all?

"This is where the property begins." Joel nodded over his shoulder to the left side of the road. "The house is just over the crest of that hill."

The rolling hills in the eastern area of the province stretched before them as they crested the hilltop. The golden hues of evening embellished the horizon and reflected across the wintry fields.

A sharp intake of breath sounded from Lydia. He slowed the horses, so she could soak in the full view. "This is like a piece of heaven on Earth."

"The house has been abandoned for some time." Joel didn't want her hopes set too high. The farmhouse required as much work as the barns and the fields. He guided the horses into the driveway.

She surveyed the closer view of the house with wide eyes. A tear glistened on the edge of her eyelashes. "I never imagined." Lydia's voice trembled, and a knot formed in Joel's stomach. He couldn't stand for her to be disappointed after she'd placed so much trust in him to come so far from her home.

He'd let her down.

"You won't have to live here until everything is fixed." Joel thought he'd explained the property's condition. Apparently, she wasn't prepared after all. Her hesitation to respond prodded him further. "I promise, Lydia, I'll make the house just how you want it to be."

"This is so much more than I dreamed. Can we go look?"

"You like it?"

"This is a storybook house. How will I ever keep from becoming prideful living in such a place?"

Laughter rippled through Joel's chest. "Hard work, my *fraw*. Hard work. The paint is peeling; the gardens are in shambles; and when you see the inside . . . well."

Lydia's cheeks were as crimson as the sunset tinging the clouds. He'd called her his *fraw*. She was his wife, but he'd spoken the words as an endearment. He'd not meant to assume such intimacy. The realization warmed his own cheeks.

"I'm not afraid of work." She descended from the wagon quickly and walked the overgrown driveway—which split the property between the house and barn—as though she would begin this very minute.

"Be careful. The entire porch needs to be replaced," Joel called while he jumped down and tethered the team to a gangly volunteer pine.

She stood staring up at the steep pitch of the gabled roof above the side porch, then walked around to the side first visible from the road. He reached her side when she was forced to stop walking due to the overgrowth between them and the building.

"I never thought I'd live in a house with a tower." She pointed at the round Victorian cupola on the far end of the house. "And three levels. What will we do with so much space?"

Most Amish fill a big house with children.

His promise to be satisfied with friendship stopped him from saying so aloud. Instead, he offered, "The house was built as a boarding school for girls. Seems right a teacher should live here."

A light sparked in those deep green eyes. One thing Joel knew about Lydia, if he knew anything, was she'd set her mind on a new idea. Like the moment she'd decided to take down the bidder at the auction, she'd seen another challenge.

"Can I name the farm?" she asked.

"Whatever you like."

"Annandale." She surveyed the house—the fields beyond to the north, the barn to the west, then south to the road with more fields and out buildings behind—and finally set him in her sights as she faced the east. "Annandale Hill. What do you think?"

He thought the vision in front of him was remarkable. He thought he owed *Gott* an enormous debt of gratitude. He thought his heart would burst.

"You disapprove. The street name caught my eye when we first arrived. Not very original, am I? It was just the first thing to come to mind."

"You've got me all wrong there, Lydia. I think Annandale Hill is perfect." The name rolled off his tongue with the ease one used to beckon an old friend.

How had he ever imagined himself here without this woman to dream alongside him? Their home would be a small taste of heaven. If only he could make her comfortable with being his wife.

A nagging conviction to tell her about Rachel ulcerated his conscience. Why hadn't he told her how recently he'd been engaged? At first, he'd proved such a terrible landlord, he hadn't wished to give her more reason to think him foolish. Later, he reasoned not to muddy the waters of an already-complicated proposal. Now, he feared pushing her further away. She'd been wary of him all day, and he'd only hinted at the topic.

If Rachel and Sarah weren't sisters . . .

If they didn't have to live with Sarah . . .

"Look, Joel!" She called from near the barn, holding a large, wooden sign over her head. "Annandale School for Girls, founded 1885."

He took her at her word. Daylight was disappearing fast. "We better head back before we're stuck in the pitch black."

Why tell her now? There was no changing what happened. He'd ruin the present with the past. The rationalization was a weak tonic against the slow bleed of the deception he was too afraid to face.

"*Ya*. All right." She lay the sign against the barn, spun around for a last look, and walked with a lightness he'd never seen in her step.

Chicken-hearted or no, he wanted to enjoy her delight a little longer. He'd tell her in time—if necessary.

CHAPTER SIX

Soft, white flour enveloped Lydia's fingers. She plunged them deeper into the large mixing bowl and massaged the shortening through the mixture. Making pies was familiar. The action soothed her nerves. From Sarah's kitchen window, Lydia could see her in-laws standing with backs turned and heads moving in animated discussion. She reached for a small pitcher of ice water to add to the pie crust mixture. Staying busy was the best distraction.

Joel was at work on their farm. Sarah barely spoke a word to her on the days she was left without Joel. Was there an unspoken custom Lydia breached to cause offense? Because for the life of her, Lydia didn't understand Sarah's coldness. When Mary was with child, she had her moments of unexplained grumpiness, but Sarah's disgruntlement was never-ending. If Lydia could just bear up until her own house was ready.

The dough came together under the pressure of her hands. Then with the gentle motion of the rolling pin, a small disc of dough stretched into a smooth circle ready for a mound of apple filling. The thought of warm, fried pies brought a bit of home with it.

The creak of the back door, followed by the stomp of boots to remove the snow from the early morning storm, indicated Sarah's return to the house.

"What are you doing?" Her sister-in-law stood, hands on hips, staring at the flat disc of dough on the floured counter.

The critical tone of the question cut into Lydia as sure as the knife she held would trim the crust into small, neat circles. *A soft answer turneth away wrath.*[1] Since Lydia had no answer, silence was more prudent. She shifted her focus to dropping a spoonful of apples on the dough rounds, then folding and crimping the edges until each made a plump half-moon ready to fry.

"Those little pies are such a waste. I've never understood the purpose when a real pie is faster and more economical." Sarah hovered over Lydia's shoulder like a hawk.

Memories of Martha Stoltzfus came to mind. Lydia had learned to deal with Martha's criticism. Martha was an elder, and she tempered her harsh opinions with good deeds, making the bitter much easier to overlook. Sarah was neither an elder nor had she shown any willingness to find anything good in Lydia at all.

"Sarah, what have I done to offend you? I truly do not know."

Sarah's lips pressed into a thin line before she whirled around to begin thumping pots down from the cabinets onto the stove. She grabbed some potatoes and, wielding a small knife, began peeling at a furious pace.

Such confounded stubbornness. And why?

Lydia suppressed the anger rising to the surface and bit back a curt remark. *A soft answer turneth away wrath.* "Please. I would ask forgiveness if I knew."

Sarah ceased peeling but didn't turn around. Her shoulders slumped. "Ask your—" Sarah closed her mouth tight.

"Ask who?"

"Joel." Sarah's refusal to call Joel Lydia's husband was evident.

---

1 Proverbs 15:1

"Do you think I am unfit for Joel? Is that the problem?"

"I will not speak of it anymore. Abe will be displeased with me."

Did Abe find his wife's uncharitable attitude better than telling the truth? Lydia clenched her jaw to refrain from asking. Besides, Abe was friendly to her.

What was Joel keeping from her? And why? She'd have to endure the silence until Joel returned.

After a long and painfully quiet meal with Abe and Sarah, Lydia trekked to the barn. Snow crunched under her feet with each lonesome step. Once again, Joel had worked past the dinner hour. His meal remained in the oven to stay warm. Lydia settled onto a bale of straw to wait for him and wished she had a book. Her favorites were still packed away. A trip to the library would no doubt be mocked by her sister-in-law as frivolous when so much work needed to be done.

If only the farmhouse renovations could be finished sooner. Perhaps tomorrow, Joel would consent to allow her to help him. He'd insisted on working alone for over a week now. She didn't understand. Two sets of hands were better than one. He seemed to enjoy her company while they worked, but lately, he left earlier each day and returned later.

A horse nickered outside. Lydia jumped to open the door. On the other side, Joel stepped down from the wagon. A look of surprise, followed by a smile, lit Joel's face when she held up her lantern. At least someone was happy to see her.

"You missed me." His eyes twinkled with the pleasure of a tease. He led the horses inside. "*Danki.* We're about frozen." He reached for Amazon and led her into the barn.

The lantern glowed brightly between them and cast long shadows across the floor. Dark circles under his eyes evidenced the long hours he'd been at work. He stepped closer and moved a hand toward her shoulder, then just as quick dropped his arm back to his side. "What brings you out here?" he asked.

How could she bring up her petty troubles to a man who worked until bone-tired, half-frozen, and hungry? "I'd thought to speak to you about something, but it's no matter. I'll help you feed the horses, so you can come inside to warm and eat."

"May as well talk while we work."

Lydia scooped grain into the feed bucket and hoped her voice wouldn't reveal the tension behind her words. "Sarah doesn't like me being here too well."

"*Ya.* I know. I'm sorry for it."

At least he hadn't denied the obvious or reprimanded her for unkind thoughts. "I asked her what I had done to cause offense. She says I have to ask you."

Joel slumped his back against a wooden beam with his head bowed as if in prayer. "I should have told you." His voice was low and quiet. "Before I came to Lancaster, I was engaged to Sarah's sister."

"You were engaged?" She wasn't surprised. He was thirty-two years old. Of course, he'd been engaged before. "I don't understand the fuss. Clearly, you weren't engaged any longer."

"Rachel broke the engagement before I went to Lancaster. Sarah blames me for not giving her sister more time. And I suppose she is disappointed at not having the company of her sister."

"What do you mean more time? How long had it been?"

"Three weeks." Joel's face contorted with misery.

He hadn't merely loved someone else before they met. The pain on his face showed how much he still did. Why did she feel like she'd been kicked by a horse?

After all, she didn't marry for love. She appreciated the boundaries Joel kept in line with their agreement to a marriage of convenience. Yet somehow, the knowledge his love belonged to another was painful. She'd begun to believe he found her special. She must have imagined the care in his actions, the tenderness in his voice. The pain in her stomach twisted. What an imagination she had.

Hay pricked through her stockings. She'd backed into the bales near the door, wishing she could hide. *No one else.* He'd said so on the crossing to the island. Why had she forgotten the warning?

When a man said no one else, he really meant he loved someone else. Had Simeon not taught her well enough? Shame washed over her. "You should go in the house. I'll stay here." She hated the crack in her voice. She couldn't even look up, or the well of tears behind her eyes would spill.

"Please. Look at me, Lydia."

Instead, she turned her back, too ashamed for him to see the feelings she had stupidly allowed her heart to develop for him.

"Lydia, please."

She waited in silence until he moved away to finish caring for Amazon.

She listened as he moved about his chores. Then, without a word, Joel came to stand behind her once more. His warmth heated her from his nearness. A nearness she foolishly desired but would never succumb to again. He'd have to wait forever before she'd turn around to face him.

At his sigh behind her, Lydia closed her eyes, and hot tears splashed against her cheeks. She shook her head in silent refusal. The quiet footfalls of his retreat stabbed her conscience. She must forgive him as she was raised to do in the Amish faith, but she needed time. She'd keep her heart on better guard from now on.

Alone, she sank to the floor and wept. What a fool. Why had she ever trusted another man? One thing was for sure and certain: she would never trust her own heart again. She curled against the bales of straw and let sleep overtake her.

Groggy and way too warm, Lydia pushed back the heavy blankets covering her. Slowly, the reality of having fallen asleep in the barn came to her. But now she was in her bed with no recollection of coming inside. The extra blankets Joel used for his bed on the floor were piled on top of her. No wonder she was so hot.

The moon shone bright through the window. Angling her wristwatch into the light, she saw the time—two o'clock. A hazy recollection of being carried from the barn during her sleep came to mind. Joel must have carried her inside and covered her up. Mortification chilled her as thoroughly as the pile of blankets had warmed her. Sarah would judge her behavior as foolish and have yet another reason to dislike her.

"Joel." She called his name softly. He'd want his blankets. The floor was cold.

He made no reply.

"Joel," she whispered louder. She may be ashamed and angry, but she didn't want him to catch pneumonia. Still, the only response was silence.

Lydia couldn't recall ever losing control of her emotions as she had in the barn. Even through the tragedy that took her sister's life and the following heartache inflicted by her beau, she'd maintained a strong outer appearance. How had she let this cause her to crumble?

The whitewashed boards above her head became clearer as her eyes adjusted to the night. Shadows danced around the space as clouds moved in and out of the moonlight. Lydia's thoughts and questions waltzed to the tempo. She'd agreed to a marriage of convenience. What did she expect? What had she truly wanted? She hadn't anticipated love, but now . . . now, she hadn't an inkling of hope. Whether Joel had resurrected hope or love in her heart, she couldn't tell. Either had clearly been unintended. She would always remain practical, necessary Lydia—never the beloved one.

Suddenly thankful Joel hadn't awakened, she leaned across the bed with a blanket to where he slept.

A bare, wooden floor was all she found. Bolting upright, she stretched across the footboard to check in front of the bed. Nothing.

Where could he be at this time of night?

She waited for him to return until a fitful sleep of worry and fear claimed her again.

Fatigue tugged Joel's eyelids. He rubbed them back open. The living room of the Annandale farmhouse came into focus, and he saw a week's worth of work to be finished by day's end. A long night of work by the light of a kerosene lantern rendered every muscle in his body taut and sore. After carrying Lydia, cold and asleep, from the barn to her bed, he'd returned to the farm, determined she wouldn't stay with Abe and Sarah another day.

Dawn was approaching. He brushed off his pants as he stood, only to watch a smear of white paint trail behind his hand onto his dark clothes. Terrific. He'd painted himself, as well as the kitchen and living area of their new house. He had to hurry if he was to get back to Abe's before Lydia awoke. Careful to avoid the tacky walls drying slowly in the cold, he stretched into his heavy coat and pulled the door closed behind him.

Amazon gave him a sleepy greeting as he untethered her in the barn. At least she knew the way. Driving a buggy in the dark wasn't a habit Joel liked to make; but since the days had grown so short and he had all the work to get done, he and Amazon were getting used to the trip. Local drivers seemed to be showing them respect on the road as well. In fact, most people had gone out of their way to make the Amish feel welcome in their community. Too bad his own kinfolk couldn't do the same for Lydia.

As Abe's place came nearer, Joel prayed for wisdom. The vision for the New Hope church district was one of unity, where the core beliefs of their Anabaptist heritage could be lived in a way that drew members closer to both *Gott* and each other. He had to keep his attitude toward Sarah in check, or else his own family could splinter into factions. The best course was to move with Lydia into their own place to keep the peace. He wasn't sure Lydia would agree, as fearful upset as she was with him now. And Sarah could take the move as a slight against her. *Oh, Gott, let all this work according to Your will.*

Light from the barn shone like a beacon to guide the horse. Abe was watching for him.

Inside the barn, Joel got out of the buggy, while Abe tethered Amazon. Joel called to Abe, "No reason to unhitch her. We'll be leaving soon enough."

Abe tilted his head toward the house. "What happened?"

Sarah burst back through the side door. "Joel Yoder! What have you done?" Sarah had always been a bit feistier than other Amish girls. At five feet tall, she was no more intimidated by the twelve inches he towered over her than if they were all still children playing in the school yard.

"Me?" Joel met his sister-in-law's icy glare. "Are you suddenly concerned for my *fraw's* feelings, or do you just want to pick a fight?" Joel regretted the fierceness of his words as soon as they left his lips. If he was aiming for peace, he was doing a poor job.

"Maybe tip-toeing around with your secrets has been the problem. I didn't lead a girl on her whole life, then finally pay her proper attention just because marrying her would get me the farm I wanted. I didn't turn around and marry a total stranger just to get a farm because the other woman actually wanted love."

"That's not the way of it." Joel's heart knew his intentions weren't as Sarah described. And yet, everything she said appeared to be true.

"You're not fooling me with this sham of a marriage. I know you sleep on the floor. You don't love Lydia any more than you ever loved Rachel." Sarah pinned him with a glare, then spun around to leave.

Abe didn't utter a word.

Even Amazon remained quiet, except for the soft clop of her hooves against the straw.

So, they all thought him incapable of truly loving a woman, wholeheartedly and unselfishly.

The worst was knowing Lydia believed he didn't love her. Did he? If the deep, aching pain he'd battled all night held any proof, he must. Joel's displeasure with Sarah was nothing compared to the agony of knowing Lydia was suffering because of his own actions or, rather, inaction.

The beautiful bay shook her black mane and tail. Joel stroked the white patch down her forehead. His brother moved alongside him, saying nothing. Abe never said much. He waited until the silence drove the other person to speak first.

"Cut it out."

"What?"

"Waiting for me to spill the beans."

Abe continued brushing Amazon in long strokes along her back. Joel never knew what his brother was thinking. This morning was no exception.

He had to get his place ready by nightfall. And then, he'd find a way to explain everything to Lydia. Rachel didn't come close to Lydia in his affections. Rachel would be the first to tell Lydia so, if she were here. She'd broken the engagement because Joel cared for her more as a sister than a wife. But how was he supposed to express his feelings for Lydia when she insisted on friendship?

Just when he thought they were making progress. Joel sure had his work cut out for him—and not only on the farm.

Heaven knew, Abe wouldn't outright ask, but his brother deserved to know Joel's plans. "I want to have the new house ready for us to stay there tonight. I'll take Lydia with me after breakfast, if she agrees."

"Lydia's not as indifferent as you may think. Just be careful, brother. I see the same longing as Rachel had all those years. She wants you but thinks she can't have you. And yet, she's your *fraw*. I don't know what secrets the two of you are keeping from each other. Don't want to know. But if you love Lydia the way I think you do, you're going to have to show her. And the two of you are going to have to talk. Secrets only cause strife." Abe spoke with the same calm rhythm as his gentle movement along the mare's barrel and flank. "I'll come help you today."

Joel couldn't remember Abe ever stringing so many words together at once. The man who hardly spoke was advising him and his wife to get talking. And this wasn't the first time Abe was more in tune with the woman's emotions than Joel. He'd foreseen Rachel's decision while Joel had been taken off-guard.

"Better to lend a hand than point a finger, *ya?*" Abe put down the brush. "We'll be wanting a *goot* breakfast then." He motioned for Joel to follow him to the house.

Joel's heart thudded against his chest. His brother was right. Even Sarah was right. He had asked Rachel to marry him for all the wrong reasons. Of course, the outward appearance was that he had done the same with Lydia. He'd searched his heart before marrying Lydia to make sure he wasn't repeating the same mistake. He thought Lydia merely needed time for love to grow. Now, he wasn't so sure. After last night, love may not stand a chance.

To love as Gott loves is always the right choice. His heart echoed back his *gammi's* advice. Could he love Lydia the way she deserved?

The sun's rays beaming through the windows of the new enclosed buggy kept Lydia warm, as she drove to Joel's farm. Would Annandale ever feel like her own? Theirs? Joel and Abe had left earlier, while she packed their few things to bring along with her. At the crest of the hill, the farm came into view and stole Lydia's breath as it had on first sight. In her mind's eye, she envisioned how a spring version might appear in a few months' time. She pictured the house with a fresh coat of paint, the gardens tilled exposing the lush, red earth and flowers to color the porch and pathways.

Annandale stood out like a wintry dream in the sunlight. A dream in desperate want of hard work. And for now, the busyness was a welcome relief to help her forget the painful revelation of the evening before. If Joel did indeed make the inside habitable by nightfall, she could escape the humiliation of any further discussions with Sarah. She tried not to give Joel too much credit for providing her own space— away from her sister-in-law—even though she was inwardly thrilled. His decision was to make their lives bearable. She reminded herself over again that Joel was not a man acting out of love toward her. He loved someone else.

The thought served as a constant reminder to keep her feet firmly planted in reality and her heart in check. No matter the messages his deep brown eyes conveyed to the contrary.

The plumber's pick-up truck still sat in the driveway, so Lydia drove the horse to the barn, not minding the extra steps to unload the buggy. She grabbed as many bags as she could with each hand. Joel would insist on helping. If she carried plenty on her way in the house, she could remain busy enough to avoid talking.

The overgrowth which had obscured the view of the house had been replaced with neat rows of stacked firewood. Their New Hope church district was still small, but all the Amish men had come on a Saturday soon after the house was purchased to help Joel clear the property. They burned or hauled away the unusable debris, then cut and stacked the rest. In the week since Lydia had been to the house, the pile had more than doubled in length and height. No wonder Joel was so tired every evening. New windows replaced the cracked and broken ones. All around her stood evidence of more work Joel had done by himself.

He sure made remaining angry with him difficult.

Forgiveness was the way of her faith. She may forgive Joel, but her own wayward heart required a tight reign. She would not relinquish it to a man who loved another. Never again.

Closer to the house, voices drifted from the direction of the kitchen entrance. Joel and the *Englisch* plumber stood by the dilapidated old wellhouse. A patchwork of boards covered the opening until a safer structure could be erected. The plumber had mentioned a neighbor with a young child. Lydia would worry until the job was finished. Throughout her tenure as a school teacher, safety was always a priority. Lydia would do anything to prevent an accident that may hurt a child. She'd never forgiven herself for failing to prevent her sister's accident.

As she turned to go the other way, a blur of red flashed behind the woodpile. A child?

"Hello?" Lydia used the English greeting, but no one answered.

She dropped the bags and hurried to the corner where she'd seen what had certainly been a small child and called again. "Hello?"

Behind the stacked logs, two small boots scuffled out of sight. Lydia ran toward the opposite end. Ahead of her, the same red-head popped out the other end of the woodpile. Such a fearless thing.

"Whoa, there!" The deep rumble of the plumber's voice stopped the little girl in her tracks. Was she his granddaughter? He scooped her up in the crook of one arm. How could she have missed the fact a little girl was with him earlier? "You must be Cait King's new wee tyke." He spoke as much to himself as to the girl.

The girl didn't make a sound. She hung like a rag doll from the man's brawny arm. Lydia had never seen a child respond to a stranger in such a way.

The man pulled his cell phone out of his pocket with his free hand and thumbed at the screen. "Cait. It's Ron. You missing a little red-haired girl about three or four years old?"

Should she rescue the helpless child from the man? Not that he seemed as though he would harm the girl. Standing aside never came naturally for Lydia, but with a small girl involved . . . Her heart beat against her chest like a broom handle whacked at a dusty rug. Surely, she should intervene.

"It's all right. I've got her." He spoke in a soothing tone to whom-ever Cait happened to be. "Up at the new folks' place on top of the hill. That's right. I don't know how she got this far, but she's safe. I'm leaving now. I'll have her to you in just a few minutes." He pressed his thumb on the phone and returned it to his pocket.

"Seems Cait King has her hands full with this one. Says the child won't say a word and can disappear in the blink of an eye. She's helped kids of all sorts over the years, but she's getting up in age. I'd say this one may need someone a bit younger to keep up." He hoisted the child up on his hip. "I'll be back with supplies." He nodded to the wellhouse. "Last thing we want is a wee one falling in there."

The implied danger stole the breath out of Lydia's chest. She watched as the plumber buckled the girl into the truck. Before he shut the door, Lydia found her voice. "What's her name?"

"Don't rightly know."

Lydia leaned toward the child. "What is your name?"

"Eeee," came the reply.

She was old enough to talk clearly. Maybe she was shy, although timidity did not seem to fit her disposition at all. Lydia suspected more was going on with the little *maydel*.

"Well, then, goodbye, Eeee." Lydia closed the door.

Two pudgy hands, followed by a tiny, upturned nose, pressed against the truck window. Red curls framed her large, brown eyes staring at something beyond Lydia's head. For the first time, Lydia realized Joel was right behind her.

The vehicle bumped along the driveway to the road. The little one didn't even have a decent coat.

CHAPTER SEVEN

Daylight hours passed too fast for the amount of work Joel wanted to accomplish. At least, the plumber had returned and boarded up the wellhouse for him. The barn sheltered Amazon well for the night. He and Lydia would remain warm in the lower level of the house. Under the circumstances, still a better option than returning to Abe's.

After supper, Joel finished a few chores in the barn and settled Amazon into a clean stall. He returned to the house and surveyed the large living space by lamplight. Heat from the woodstove began to knock the chill from his bones. The only furniture consisted of two simple chairs. In one, Lydia hunched over a needle and thread illuminated by her own small lantern. A couple of sleeping bags lay by the stove.

He was sorry she had to live in such rough conditions. He'd clear out the upstairs bedrooms and paint them tomorrow. For now, he hoped being in her own home was enough to show he cared for her. Just when he thought Lydia may be coming to understand their marriage meant more to him than mere convenience, Sarah had filled her mind with doubts.

Ach, he couldn't lay all the blame at Sarah's feet. He should have explained about Rachel from the start. More than anything, he yearned for Lydia's trust. Joel shook his head at the thought of his own foolishness. He'd done the opposite of proving himself trustworthy to her.

Gott, help me become the man she needs.

Joel sat in the chair opposite his wife. She hadn't looked at him. Lines of concentration crossed her brow, and her eyes focused steadily on the rhythmic work of her fingers along a piece of cloth the color of the island pines.

He leaned back and balanced on the back two legs of his chair while stretching his own. Clearing his throat, he watched for an acknowledgment of his presence from Lydia, to no avail. He tried again. Her face remained unchanged. Her sewing never paused.

"Thank you for warming the sleeping bags." He was rewarded with a dip of her head, as he carried his bedding to the far side of the room. Too bad he hadn't ordered mattresses the last time he was in the small town for supplies. His priority list was growing by the minute.

"*Goot* night, Lydia." Joel curled up to keep his shoulders inside the cover and drifted asleep to the crackle and hiss of the fire.

Awakened by the smell of bacon and the pop of hot grease, Joel's stomach rumbled with anticipation. In the kitchen, he cupped his hands under the kitchen faucet and splashed cold water on his face. A shiver ran across his chest at the chill of the drips from his new beard.

"*Goot mariye.*" Lydia handed him a towel, then grabbed another to pull a hot stack of pancakes out of the warming side of the oven.

Good morning? Joel returned the greeting, even as his hope raised a notch at the change since the previous evening. Spying the ready-made *kaffi*, he poured and carried a steaming cup for each of them to a makeshift dining table, where their two sole chairs now sat.

"You have *wunderbaar* timing," Lydia said as she set down their plated breakfast.

She sat, and then Joel bowed his head for their silent thanksgiving. As Joel opened his eyes, he looked across the table at Lydia, whose bowed head drooped low until her chin almost touched her chest. A peek into the living area revealed her sleeping bag packed into a neat roll. Had she slept at all?

"Lydia." He spoke softly, so as not to startle her.

"Hmm?" Her head bobbed, followed by a little shake. She cleared her throat and said a quiet amen before opening her eyes. She reached for her coffee and raised the cup to her lips. Her eyes met his again. "What?"

"Did you not sleep?"

"Maybe a little in the chair . . . after I finished." Her face lit with excitement, despite the tired shadow under her eyes. "I made a coat for the little girl. Did you see what she was wearing? I thought we might be able to visit the plumber. Maybe he knows where she lives." A sudden uncertainty masked the former spark in her green eyes.

Did she suppose he might think badly of her helping the *Englischer*? She'd remained up all night to help the child. If anything, he cared for her more, not less. She was a beautiful mystery. How could a woman who showed so much love for a child she didn't even know remain without a husband and family so long?

"The only thing I noticed was her hair." Joel had never seen a head covered in such a pile of red curls. And the remembrance of her so wild and free was a happy thought. "If you believe she can use a better coat, we will find a way to deliver it to her."

"*Danki*, Joel." Her hand slid across the table toward his and stopped short of touching him.

The desire to reach out to her stirred. But he held back. He should win her trust back first. He'd been so careful to keep his distance even before the revelation about Rachel—mostly because he couldn't trust himself to keep his promise if he got too close.

"Lydia." He caught her green eyes with his and continued before she looked away. "I'm sorry. The last thing I ever want to do is hurt you. I am deeply sorry for not telling you about Rachel. Words can't pay for the pain I've caused. I pray I'll never you hurt you again."

She held his gaze for a brief moment, then looked down. "I forgave you as I worked in the night, but I am thankful you asked."

"*Danki*, Lydia, for your forgiveness." Joel had felt the absence of animosity. She made breakfast and sat to eat with him. Her forgiveness was real and tangible—a gift from God and the heart of a kind and lovely woman. Yet her manners were reserved. She freely gave her forgiveness, but the easy way between them was lost. He'd shattered her trust, and he longed to restore the friendship they had begun to share.

She pushed her hands against the table to stand.

He reached out to stop her, then dropped his hand immediately. "I want to be your friend again. May I have another chance, please?"

Lydia bit her lower lip. Her fingers trembled as she smoothed her apron. Was she so frightful? Or did she feel the same spark he did when their hands touched?

He stood before she could reject his request. "I'll get the morning chores done as quickly as possible. There's a storm coming, but we should have time." The warmth from the contact of her hand still lingered as he walked to the door. He fisted his traitorous hand to wring out the memory. Lydia expected him to keep his distance. "Get some rest. We'll go when I come back," he said without looking back.

The subtle shadows of pre-dawn lit his path. Soft flakes of snow flurried in the air. The barn required as much work as the house. He'd do what he could in the barn, so Lydia could rest until the *Englisch* world awakened.

At least he hadn't purchased any livestock yet. His church allowed tractors and other mechanical farm equipment, or else he'd have more horses to keep warm. As it was, Amazon was alone in the barn for the time being.

By the mare's stall, he kicked the water trough. Ice cracked and splashed open a hole where Amazon could get a drink. He caught sight of his powerful beauty lying still and awkward on the floor. Alarm bells rang in his head. He approached her gently, praying she was not ill. Her ears perked up at his voice, but she remained otherwise motionless. The morning light was too dim to see clearly. Joel's knees popped as he knelt for a closer examination. Warmth penetrated through his glove as he stroked her. She wasn't too cold, for sure.

He reached for an odd contortion underneath the heavy blanket covering her mid-section. Amazon snorted a warning at him. He backed off.

The shape reminded him of a new colt curled by its mother. What in the world? He fetched a flashlight, which shone into the stall to reveal the mystery—the tangled curls of a red-haired little girl cocooned in Amazon's instinctual protection.

A blood-curdling wail jolted Lydia awake. For a moment, she believed the cry was her sister in another nightmare. The sound pitched higher and louder until Lydia was fully awake. She sprinted to the front door. On the porch, she found Joel, pale-faced and carrying the red-haired little girl. She was reaching, double-fisted, over his shoulder toward the barn.

Snow was falling fast and heavy. Joel's inch-deep tracks trailed from the direction of the barn. "Can you take her while I hitch up the buggy?" Joel's voice was scarcely audible over the child's continued crying. "I have to hurry, or this snow is going to make getting her home impossible. I found her with Amazon. Don't know how long she was in there, but Amazon kept her warm. She's been wailing worse than a colt torn away from its *mamm* since I brought her out of the barn."

"*Kumm, liebling.* We'll get your coat, and then we can go back to the horse." Lydia stood beside Joel, leaning around his shoulder to see the child's face. At the mention of the horse, the girl stretched her arms toward the barn again "*Ya,* I mean, yes. I'll take you to see the horse. You must put on a coat first." At the promise, the girl fell into Lydia's outstretched arms.

Joel jogged back to the barn. When Lydia stepped into the house, a new round of protests erupted from the child in her arms. Lydia wrestled the coat she made over flailing arms and an arched back. *Thank you, Gott, for allowing me to finish this coat last night.*

Lydia grabbed her own coat and two scarves, one to cover her own head and another for the girl. "Now, we can see the horse."

The crying stopped, and Lydia realized that in all the noise, the girl had not spoken a single word.

"What is your name, dear one?"

"Eeee."

Could she hear? She had understood the word horse. At least to Lydia, it seemed she had. Lydia recalled the plumber mentioned the girl never spoke at her foster home, either.

Oh, liebling, what would you say to us if you could? Lydia pulled the small girl closer to her side, as a fierce protectiveness overcame her. The child had come to them twice in the space of a day. Did she need them? Once they were all inside, Joel wrapped a heavy buggy robe around them. With the child on her lap and the soft, faux fur blanket around them, she was in no more danger of getting cold than a bear taking a winter nap. Joel slid into the seat beside her and covered his lap with the remaining end of the blanket.

Little hands stroked the fur-like underside, her fingers weaving in and out of sight through the thick layer. She pulled it against her face and nestled her cheek in its softness. Lydia's heart squeezed at the sight so innocent and pure.

She caught Joel watching, too; then his eyes met Lydia's. A white puff of air escaped past his lips as a gentle smile formed. Lydia's heart squeezed harder. He looked away, then back to Amazon, also blanketed warmly from the falling snow.

The normal trot of hooves and steady rumble of the buggy was muted by a dense layer of snow already covering the road.

"I think we better stop at the first neighbor and ask to use the phone. I'm not sure we will make it to the plumber in this weather." Joel nodded toward a light in the distance and the farm of their closest neighbor.

"*Ya.* I think so, too. Do you think she lives there? Maybe he just assumed we knew."

How far could the child have wandered? That the closest farm was her home made the most sense. The thought of the child living so near was a happy one. Her presence lit a lantern of hope and home in Lydia's heart, as though they belonged together.

"Maybe he expected we knew our neighbors already." Joel paused. "I should have made more effort. I just thought . . . "

Lydia could finish the thought, even though he did not. His wife should be with him for such introductions.

"I understand if you're not comfortable introducing me as your wife to strangers." Lydia wasn't sure of the response she hoped Joel would make, but his definitive silence was more concerning than outright admittance. She edged further away, but there was not far to go.

"*Nay,* Lydia. I thought you should have time to settle first. That is all."

The low light of the rising sun behind the clouds guided their way. An eerie absence of early morning sounds made the crunch of snow under the buggy wheels louder. A light flickered in a farmhouse window as they reached the bottom of the hill.

Joel brought the buggy to a stop. "I'll go. Will you be all right?" His eyes pointed to the girl and raised back to Lydia in silent question.

"*Ya.* We are warm."

A puff of wind and a smattering of snowflakes blew across her cheeks as the buggy door opened and closed behind Joel.

The door opened; then after a moment, he motioned for Lydia to come. Carrying the child in her arms, Lydia bent her head to cut the sting of the wind and snow on her skin.

"Quickly! Come in." A woman's voice called to them. Joel's hand rested protectively on her shoulder as he entered behind her.

"I'm Cait King." The woman held out a hand to Lydia. In her nightclothes and a fuzzy, pink robe, Cait appeared about sixty and had short gray hair and bright blue eyes. She reached for the girl. "Oh, Jessamyn." Her voiced cracked, and her misted eyes looked into Lydia's. "I've only just gotten up. I didn't even know she was gone."

Jessamyn. Lydia's head swirled. "Her name's Jessamyn?"

"Her legal name is Jessamyn, but she won't answer to it."

The child touched Lydia's cheek and said, "Mm-Eee."

Lydia's heart melted at the girl's gentle touch. "Yes, that's you."

She shook her head. "S-s-aa Mm-ee."

"Samy?"

A full smile spread across her freckled face as the little one wrapped her arms around Lydia's neck. She held on as if she never wanted to let go. If Lydia had a choice, she'd never let her go, either.

Lydia stroked the girl's curls and whispered into her ear, snuggled so close. "Samy, Joel and I have to go home because of the storm. You stay here, and we will bring the horse to see you again soon. Okay?"

The child buried her face into Lydia's chest.

Mrs. King winced. "You must be thinking we are unkind for her to run off. She's only just come to us and hardly knows us yet. They sent her to us because we have been foster parents for over thirty years. Seems no one else has been able to keep her from running away."

"Samy. Everything will be all right." How could she make the child stay when she could barely stand to leave her?

The *Englisch* woman did appear kind. The house was warm and clean, which was more than could be said of her own home in its current state of disrepair.

A Christmas tree stood just beyond the foyer. "Can you show me the pretty tree, *liebling*?" Lydia crouched down to set Samy's feet on the floor. Holding her hand, they walked to the tree.

Behind her, Joel spoke to Mrs. King. "I could install a simple chain-lock on your outside doors where she couldn't reach them."

"We thought of that, but my husband fears it may be unsafe in case of a fire."

"I see." Disappointment laced his reply. He cared. His concern for Samy was genuine, making Lydia slightly weak in the knees. A man like Joel should be a father. Why had he ever agreed to a marriage of convenience?

A tug on her sleeve drew Lydia's attention back to Samy. A chubby finger pointed at a wooden rocking horse ornament. "Eee. Eee."

"Horsey?"

"Eeeee!" A smile lit Samy's face at Lydia's understanding.

Lydia looked over her shoulder to Mrs. King, whose attention was on Samy and the tree. "I believe she is drawn to our horse. Perhaps sometime, she could . . ." Lydia glanced at Joel, who nodded agreement. "She could come to visit with us and see the horse."

"That would be lovely," the older woman agreed.

"We don't mean to be unfriendly, but the snow is coming down quick," Joel said.

Lydia stood. "*Ya.* We must be going. I hope we see you soon."

Samy ran for the door, but Cait King swooped the girl up in her arms. The pout of her lips threatened to turn to a cry.

"We thank you for getting her back to us safely." The woman opened the door for them.

Joel's gloved hand guided Lydia from behind with a gentle nudge.

Outside, Samy's wails rang from behind the closing door. Joel turned back, staring hard at the house. He looked down at Lydia with sadness in his eyes. "What can we do?"

She had no answer. He expected no reply.

Lydia's heart may as well have been wrung from her chest, as to endure the sound of Samy's screams and the sight of Joel's stricken face.

She'd vowed long ago never to be so powerless again. She'd left Lancaster to ensure control of her life. Yet, here she was helpless. She could no more rescue Samy than she had been able to save her own sister.

Back in the buggy, the cries still echoed in Lydia's ears. She leaned toward Joel and allowed herself the indulgence of his strength.

His arm slid across her shoulders, drawing her closer. "We can pray, Lydia. *Gott* loves Samy, too. He will show us what to do." His beard brushed softly against her temple. So quickly the moment passed; yet the warmth lingered, while a calm assurance settled in her soul. His nearness, along with his words in tune to the very beat of her own heart, stirred her. She had to reign in her feelings.

Joel stopped the buggy in front of the barn door. The deafening silence of a world covered in snow surrounded them. Under the heavy buggy robe, his body turned to face her. His brown eyes gently searched her face. Was admiration in the warmth that shone there? Her breath hitched.

"What I saw in you today, Lydia . . . " He swallowed, and his eyes glimmered with wetness. "I saw the love of a woman who ought to be a *mamm.*"

He was wrong. So very wrong.

"*Nay*, Joel." The explanation hung in her mouth, refusing to be said. How could she share her shame? If he knew, he'd never believe she should be a mother. Someone would take her child away, just like Samy had been taken from her parents.

Unbidden tears spilled down her cheeks. The back of Joel's hand tenderly wiped down her cheek and swept away the moisture. His touch paused at her chin, bidding her to look at him. Instead, she reached for the buggy door and fled to the safe distance of the house.

Joel intended to express admiration for a quality he believed noble. He knew Lydia took their pledge of a marriage of convenience serious and literal. Somehow, he never expected a sincere compliment to cause so much harm. Had he undone every hope of restoring their friendship by suggesting she would make a *goot* mother? By the manner in which she fled from the buggy to the house, he must have.

She was a mystery. A courting man would quit the quest for love at this point. Only Joel wasn't courting Lydia. He was married to her already. And truth be told, he was far too in love with the woman to quit, even if wedding vows didn't bind him to her. Any hope of preserving his heart from her control slipped away as he'd watched her soothe Samy. His heart flipped at the memory of the two huddled by the Christmas tree. What could make motherhood such a fearful thing for a woman so full of love for children?

Amazon's muscles shuddered beneath the towel in his hand as he skimmed over the length of her back. "Too bad you can't tell me what goes on in the mind of a strong and beautiful woman." Amazon pawed a hoof in the fresh straw and nodded her head. A smile curved his lips in response to her antics. "I'm afraid you're the only female I know how to please."

Was that it? He was the problem. It made no sense that Lydia would fear motherhood. She must find him repulsive as anything other than a friend.

Disappointment seeped through him. He touched his beard. He hadn't spent much effort in grooming of late. An Amish man must not be overly concerned with his appearance, but he'd not even run a comb through his hair this morning. He jammed his hat down further on his head. What a sight he must have made when he removed it at the neighbors' house.

"I might take a look at myself in one of those large mirrors left hanging in the house." A trim of his hair or even a good brushing was no doubt overdue. Joel looked at Amazon, who shook her head at him. "You're right. Lydia's not so shallow. Something else is troubling her." *Maybe that I'm crazy enough to talk to a horse.*

The sweet smell of grain met Joel as he opened a new feed sack and poured the contents into a storage bin. The mare whinnied. "Don't worry. I'm coming." In addition to his penchant for talking to his horse, Joel knew he had faults aplenty. After all, one fiancée wouldn't even move to Prince Edward Island for him. Now, his wife was afraid to have children. Was that it? She didn't believe he'd make a *goot datt*?

The munch of Amazon eating her oats pounded in his ears. The sound blurred into a long-ago memory of his own *datt* sitting on a stool to milk a cow while Joel held the feed bag for her to eat. Joel had known the ache of the fatherless. He'd been so young when his father died, leaving him with very few memories.

Datt Nafziger treated Joel as his own when he married his *mamm*. Even so, the sting of loss still haunted his dreams on occasion. This morning, he'd wanted nothing more than to erase that same pain from little Samy's heart.

His stomach growled a reminder that breakfast was long past. He couldn't bring himself to join Lydia in the house. Not yet. He'd work until the ache of the revelation diminished.

The snow hindered any outside work. He could pass time improving the property's outbuildings. He had claimed the building near the house for the barn, even though it was twice the size required for Amazon and their buggies, plus a milk cow he planned to purchase in the spring. The other buildings would serve for hay and farm equipment.

Walking to the other side, he took in the dimensions. Truly, he was blessed to have such a surplus of space. He pushed out thoughts of the house large enough for a quiver full of children and focused on the building in front of him.

He'd promised Lydia a new shop. Could he make half of this building suitable? As the Amish community grew, *Englischers* would be on the look-out for little places to shop, as was common in Lancaster. Being near the house would be convenient for her.

He'd make it work and prove, at the very least, that he was a man of his word.

Lydia hadn't intended to snoop. When Joel stayed in the barn past lunch, she kept busy on the second floor in what she hoped would serve as their separate bedrooms. After a thorough cleaning, the rooms were ready to paint. As the prime coat dried, she'd begun to sort their belongings and move them into the rooms.

Joel's room to the left of the stairs overlooked the wintry fields sloping down the hill into the pine forest at the property's edge. Her own room on the opposite side rendered a view of the road and the distant, snow-covered farms beyond their own. Some antique and mostly dilapidated furniture was left on the third floor as well as in the attic. She rescued a couple serviceable chairs, end tables, and one dresser to function as temporary pieces in each room.

The paint was slow to dry in the cold, so unpacking seemed the thing to do. She only meant to place Joel's Bible on the small table in his room. Then as she carried the black leather-bound pages, the wear and creases roused her curiosity. The pages' discoloration proved the many times their edges had been turned to open. The inside cover was inscribed to Abram Yoder in a script she recognized from the letter Joel's grandmother had written.

Lydia knew the look of a well-loved book. She possessed many. What she'd never owned was her own Bible. Seeing the obvious devotion to this one, she wondered what she had missed. Her bishop wasn't thrilled when members read the Bible for themselves, but he had never shunned anyone for the practice. Lydia hadn't seen a reason to push him, either.

Once again, Lydia realized she knew little of the man who was now her father-in-law and bishop of the area church. Did he approve of Joel's apparent prolific Bible reading? Or did he believe only the bishop and ministers should study the Scriptures?

A bang downstairs indicated Joel had come in the door. Lydia laid the Book down and left the room, clean and ready for him tonight.

Joel stood at the kitchen sink, washing his face and hands. He stared at his reflection in the window with a disapproving scowl. His fingers raked through his hair first and then his beard. "It's no wonder." He muttered under his breath.

"No wonder what?"

He turned with a start. "I didn't see you there."

"*Ya.* I gathered as much." She attempted to hold back a laugh, but his sheepish expression combined with his wayward hair was too much.

"Am I that funny-looking?"

"*Kumm* and sit. I found my sharp scissors this afternoon."

Joel did as she asked. Soon with a comb and scissors in hand, she would have him trimmed and tidy. She hadn't reckoned how the softness of his hair in her fingers would tempt her until she gathered a strip to cut. He sat rigid, and she wondered what she'd been thinking to suggest a haircut. She blew out a breath. Trimming her nephews' hair had never been this difficult.

As she neared the end, both of them relaxed a degree. A run-through with the comb and she was finished. "There. I hope you'll like it."

"What about the front?" Joel's inquisitive brown eyes caught her before she could look away, as she had managed so far.

She'd have to get so close to his face. So very close.

"All you have to do is clean it up a smidgen. Can't hurt it any."

She reached down. To get close enough, her legs pressed against his. "Joel, I . . . " She stepped back.

"I trust you. With all those delicate quilts and crafts you make, I know you can make it straight."

She may as well get this over with. His warm breath heated her face and neck as she worked. He smelled of soap and hard work. He took her hand when she finished, and her insides quivered. With his other hand, he removed the comb and scissors, then held both her hands.

When he stood over her, she couldn't tear her gaze away from his brown eyes searching deep into her. She saw kindness and concern laced with a question she couldn't decipher.

"If you believe I would not be a *goot datt,* you can tell me. I'll do whatever it takes to become the man I need to be."

"Oh, Joel. I've never thought such a thing." He had this all wrong.

"Samy needs a home. Whether she or *Gott* has chosen us, I'm not sure." He lifted her hands to his chin. The softness of his lips caressed her knuckles. "Will you pray with me for *Gott's* will for Samy, even so far as to offer our home to her?"

She'd never been asked to know *Gott's* will, only to accept it. Joel had no idea of the fear his request invoked. Yet how could she say no while the fresh memory of Samy's tears still tore at her heart? "Will we find *Gott's* answer in the Bible?"

"*Ya.* If we seek with an open heart, He will show us. We would have to apply to become foster parents or to adopt. Some in our district back in Ontario have adopted through the foster system. *Datt* and *Mamm* can help us understand the process. But *Gott* will determine our steps."

She'd failed Louisa. If she'd been with a man like Joel instead of Simeon, how different everything might have been. Once again, she recalled Samy's small arms wrapped around her and relived the desperate cries. She would not turn her back this time. "I will pray with you."

CHAPTER EIGHT

Late May, 2017

Annandale Hill, Prince Edward Island

Joel had begun to believe spring had settled in for an extraordinarily long winter's nap. April snows kept him at work indoors until he had little left to do. May had finally thawed the earth enough to plow. He breathed in the smell of freshly tilled soil. The rows promised sight of ribbons of new life. Next week, he'd begin planting. Once the hot sun of summer burned upon his back, he'd recall these days and cherish the heat all the more. So he supposed today.

The long winter was a blessing in the barn, where he'd re-created Lydia's Amish Shoppe. He hadn't revealed his work to her yet. He'd saved the surprise for when he finished. When *Datt* Nafziger requested they host this Sunday's church meeting, he decided it was the perfect time to use the space and surprise Lydia as well. She knew he'd prepared the barn to host a gathering, but he'd not let her in to see the true purpose of his work.

He scraped mud from his boots, then removed them before going in the house to avoid creating more work for Lydia. Tomorrow, they would host their first church meeting. His mother and sister-in-law, Sarah, were coming to help her. He knew Lydia had scrubbed, dusted, and polished every inch of floor and furnishings at least once, if not twice, already. He'd wondered how freshly painted walls could need cleaning. Apparently, Lydia could see spider webs invisible to him. She'd swatted one away as an answer to his inquiry.

If he wanted to show her the shop before his family arrived, he had to hurry. He poked his head through the door. When he didn't see Lydia in the kitchen, he went inside to find her. A draft blew against his back, and the door slammed behind him.

"Joel?" Lydia called from upstairs.

"It is me. Do you have a minute?" he hollered back toward the staircase. "I would like to show you something." His volume decreased with the last words as Lydia stepped into view at the bottom of the stairs.

"I think so. Do you know what time they're coming?" Her nervousness at having Sarah's help seeped into the question. He hoped his mother's presence would temper Sarah's harshness. But Lydia had no way of knowing what to expect. *Mamm* had only returned from Ontario a few weeks ago.

"Soon, I think. But I have a surprise for you first."

Her left brow raised in question as she came to stand in front of him. "Outside?"

"In the barn." He handed her the jacket she kept on the peg and opened the door. "We have to go around to the side door, facing the road. But wait for me. And close your eyes."

She stopped and faced him. Curiosity sparked in her eyes. Joel kept his expression neutral. At least, he hoped he did. But inside, he thrilled with the hope of impressing her. For months, he'd worked secretly to create an image identical to the shop she had shaped out of his grandparents' old farmhouse. Doing so in a run-down, former dairy shed was no easy task. "You have to close your eyes, Lydia."

With a sigh of resignation, she complied. He slid his hand into hers, noting the softness against his calloused palm. As he began to walk, she placed her hand more firmly in his. He'd have to surprise her more often.

Stopping in front of the sign he had just put up that morning, he took her shoulders to turn her toward the sign at the roadside entrance.

A black SUV crested the hill, slowed down, and turned into the driveway beside them.

"What's that?" Eyes still closed, Lydia felt for his hand.

"A car. I don't know why it's here." Joel turned her away from the sign. "I guess you better open your eyes." He couldn't withhold the disappointment from his voice. "Try not to look at the barn, if you can help it."

"All right."

They both stood staring at the SUV and the young woman who got out. She was probably lost, looking for directions. So, why did the moment feel like the life-changing kind? For good. For bad. He couldn't tell.

Lydia hadn't let go of his hand. Did she feel the foreboding as well?

"Can I help you?" he called, not wanting to leave Lydia's side or let go of her hand so that he may.

The woman didn't seem inclined to come closer to them either. "Are you Joel and Lydia Yoder?"

"*Ya.* We are."

"I'm a social worker from Child Services. May I speak with you?"

"Of course."

Someone needed to approach the lady; but next to him, Lydia felt more immovable than ever. He looked at her. Her face was ashen. In his hand, hers felt moist and cold. "Do you want me to go alone to speak to this woman?" He spoke only for her to hear.

She looked at him. Her eyes wide.

He squeezed her hand. "Everything is all right." Was it? Yet he assured her anyway. "*Kumm*, Lydia. Let's see what she wants."

Once before, Lydia had felt her life shift as she felt it now. The day an officer in a black police car brought news that shattered her family and all her dreams. But this couldn't be such news. She had no sister to wander away while she was distracted by her beau. No beau to urge her to let a little girl out of her sight. If she loved him, he said, she'd pay him at least as much attention as she did her sister. Why had she listened?

Would the past never leave her alone?

"*Kumm*." She heard him say. "It will be all right."

"*Nay!*" She wanted to shout, but no sound came out.

"Lydia. *Vass is letz?*"

Joel?

She was with Joel Yoder, not Simeon Glick. Worry creased his brow. His brown eyes searched hers.

"I'm sorry."

"Don't' be. Stay close to me," he said. She felt his fingers intertwine tightly around her own.

"I'm fine." Her wobbling voice was less than assuring. She removed her hand from his and repeated, "I'm fine, really." She was firmly planted in reality again, though the déjà vu moment left her rattled.

Behind the car, plumes of smoke escaped from the chimney, fading into the air that drifted over the fields and down the hills beyond. She was far from her past, here on her hilltop home. She'd come as far as she ever hoped to get.

She raised her hand to signal to the woman that they were coming. The woman looked up the hill to them and nodded before turning to look in the backseat window of her car. Whatever was in there, the woman was not moving away from it. Instead she held an outstretched hand toward them. "I'm Traci Holbrook."

Lydia shook Traci's hand. "Would you like to come inside?"

Traci stepped back and tilted her head toward the car. "I have someone with me. That's why I'm here." Traci's eyes cut over to Joel, then back to Lydia. "We have a foster child in need of an emergency foster family. Her previous foster parents urged us to come here. I've been told you know the child, and they feel she would be happier here than anywhere else. We have reviewed your recent application, home study, and completed courses. We only have to finish some necessary paperwork."

"Samy?"

"Yes. Mrs. King is . . . Well, she is unable to care for the girl right now. I cannot give specifics for confidentiality reasons."

Lydia had just visited the Kings last week, as she had every week since Christmas. Cait knew they hoped to adopt Samy someday. The Kings could not adopt Samy, and Cait was pleased to know she might have a permanent home. But Cait hadn't mentioned anything about such an abrupt change. What could have gone wrong?

"Can you come in with the child?" Joel asked. "We should have this discussion where it's warm."

"I suppose. Although, I'm afraid she may not want to leave you once she goes in the house."

"Well, then, she won't have to," Joel replied with authority.

Traci's eyes widened in surprise. "That would be the ideal solution, Mr. Yoder. But there is the matter of paperwork and agreements."

"*Kumm.* Bring Samy. We will continue inside." Joel was already walking away, expecting them to follow.

"It's the Amish way. He knows no different." Lydia explained the manners that appeared odd to Traci. "For sure, it makes no sense to stand in the cold and talk when there's a warm fire in the house." Lydia smiled. "May I help Samy out of the car?"

After a nod from Traci, Lydia opened the car door. A blur of red curls toppled out as Samy ran straight to Lydia and clung to her skirt.

Down at knee-height, Samy's red curls sunk into the fabric of Lydia's dress. Two little arms wrapped around Lydia's legs, almost throwing her off-balance. Only the soft green color of her coat remained visible as she pressed closer. Lydia reached for the small hands gripping the back of her legs, then knelt down to Samy's level. "I'm happy to see you, too, *liebling.*"

Sapphire blue eyes gazed up at her before flitting away toward the barn. "Eeee?" The question came in the only sound Samy ever made and which labeled almost everything.

"Yes, we will visit the horsey." She pressed the little fingers into hers with a gentle touch to regain Samy's attention. "But first, we must go to the house. All right?"

Samy took off toward the porch where Joel waited.

How could life change so quickly?

"I can see why Mrs. King was so insistent," Traci said to her. "And truth be told, Mrs. Yoder, we have no one else who will take her."

The social worker would have a different opinion if she knew what happened to Louise. And why.

I know, my child, and I have brought her to you. The words resonated from a place deep within herself—a part of her being only *Gott* could reach—a heart whisper. Would He truly entrust a child to her care? Doubt edged into her thoughts. There was no forgiveness for what she had done. But Joel was a man who could be trusted. God must have brought Samy to him.

After a long morning of paperwork, Samy was indeed living with Joel and Lydia. The arrangement was temporary until the court awarded custody. Lydia had almost no time to absorb the shock before her in-laws arrived to help prepare for church service at the farm tomorrow. So now, she lingered on the edge of her bed, where Samy finally slept, covered snugly in blankets and a quilt. The dim glow of lantern light illuminated the bedside in the room Lydia claimed for her own. From the upstairs bedroom window, the last moments of daylight disappeared from the horizon. The voices of her in-laws mingled with Joel's from the living area below. Lydia's own voice was weary from singing hymn after hymn until Samy succumbed to sleep. She rose, careful not to disturb the little one, and tiptoed to the door.

Sarah stood waiting at the top of the stairs. "Is she asleep yet?" she asked, not too quietly.

Lydia pulled the door closed and hurried to the steps. "At last," Lydia whispered in a hint and started down the stairs.

Sarah didn't follow. Over her shoulder, Lydia could see her peeking in each room. *Of all the busy-body . . .*

"How convenient that you have a room already made up for the child." Sarah shot an accusatory glance Lydia's way.

"Please, let's not wake her." Lydia headed downstairs, refusing the bait. Was Sarah suggesting she knew about the marriage agreement? Her stomach knotted at the possibility.

Sarah could find any number of uses for such information, all of which would make Lydia's life miserable. Lydia had escaped the shame and humiliation of being husbandless in one community. Was she to endure the same here?

The stair curved into the living area entrance. Joel and Abe sat across from *Mamm* and *Datt* Nafziger, each holding Dutch Blitz playing cards. Lydia crossed the polished wood floor and stopped directly behind Joel. In a motion she hoped looked habitual and unplanned, she rested her hands on his shoulders. She'd never freely touched Joel in such a manner. He startled, and his shoulders flinched. Embarrassed, Lydia pulled away, but he reached up to keep her right hand in place. The warmth that surged through her from his hand crept all the way to her cheeks, which was not a reaction she desired Sarah to see.

The bishop looked to his wife. What must he think? She'd never behaved so immodestly. But *Mamm* Nafziger's lip curved up in response to their silent communication.

"Makes a father's heart light to see his son happy with his *fraw*. And a bishop glad to oversee a happy marriage." *Datt* Nafziger smiled.

Oh, dear. She couldn't look him in the eye. He wasn't reprimanding her. He was giving his consent to her behavior. What had she done? She'd essentially lied to the bishop and his wife.

She looked away to find Sarah watching. Then with the last ounce of boldness she could muster, she bent to speak in Joel's ear. Her *kapp* brushed his temple. He leaned his ear closer so that her lips nearly touched him. *"Danki."*

She wanted to say more, but the intimacy had stolen her breath. She backed away, hopeful he understood.

Joel moved aside and patted the half of a seat that opened beside him. As graceful as possible, she wedged into the small space. Their shoulders touched, and he whispered in her ear this time. "My pleasure, Lydia."

Across from them, Abe's cheeky grin turned flat under the hovering stare of his wife's displeasure.

"I think it's time for us to leave." Sarah beckoned her husband.

Everyone slowly filed into the kitchen, as Abe and Sarah draped on layers of coats, gloves, shawls, and head coverings. *Mamm* and Bishop Nafziger didn't seem to notice anything untoward as they said goodbye to Sarah and Abe. And Joel casually put a fresh pot of *kaffi* on the stove.

Hatred stirreth up strifes: but love covereth all sins.[2] The proverb described the short time she had spent with the Nafzigers. Lydia had already witnessed their long-suffering attitudes of grace and patience toward others. If Samy could grow up in such a home . . .

Tears burned at the back of Lydia's eyelids at the thought, which she worded into a silent prayer for the precious child.

Datt Nafziger headed back to the living area. "No need to let a good game go unfinished." He rapped his cards on the table as he spoke. "Lydia can play Abe's hand."

As they headed back to the game table, Joel caught her eye and winked.

Mamm followed with a plate of cookies. "You don't mind, do you, Lydia? No one will miss just four from Sabbath dinner tomorrow."

Lydia snitched one from the plate. "Not at all."

In fact, fresh whoopie pies made the perfect end to this *wunderbaar-goot* day. She wished the joy could continue forever. An inner warning reminded her how the balance of her present happiness hung upon too many secrets and deceptions.

In front of each player, *Mamm* Nafziger delivered a steamy cup of coffee. Lydia dunked her cookie before taking the first bite. The softened chocolate melted away on her tongue.

Gone too soon.

Joel watched Lydia's eyelids droop as they waved goodbye to his folks. Nothing about this long day had gone as he would have predicted. With Samy asleep upstairs, everything had changed. Months of prayer led to this day. Samy's presence in their home was no accident, but a part of *Gott's* plan for all of their lives. Now, more than ever, he and Lydia needed to be united to provide the security of a family for Samy. But he was as much at a loss in how to move beyond friendship with his *fraw* as he had ever been.

"What were you going to show me this morning?" Lydia's voice broke into his thoughts. She pointed toward the barn. "Can we see it now?"

Keeping the women away from the shop had been a difficult task all day. *Datt* and Abe helped, as they understood his desire to show Lydia alone before anyone else.

"You're tired. We'll go first thing before chores. Will that be all right?" Joel didn't want to disappoint her, but he knew how exhausted she was.

"Whatever you think. Makes no never mind to me. I am tired, but what a day! I can hardly believe Samy is to live with us. For now."

Did Joel hear disappointment or resignation in her voice? "I don't believe *Gott* has brought her here to let her be taken away."

"Traci said we must be prepared for the possibility." Lydia sounded as though she had little hope. Yet Joel was buoyed by today's events. He was sorry for whatever circumstance had befallen the Kings to bring Samy to them. But he was certain *Gott* was working all things according to His plan.

Joel led her into the living room. "Are you too tired to pray with me before going to bed?"

"After all *Gott* has done today, I want nothing more than to pray with you this evening." She sat at the small table where they'd prayed every day since finding Samy in the barn. She eyed his Bible still on the table from the previous evening. "Would you read a Psalm to me?"

Joel would never tire of the routine. More than Lydia's whispers in his ear or the touch of her hands this evening, her reverence and devotion drew him now. Their quiet moments in prayer were among his greatest pleasures. She shied away from reading the Scripture herself, but asked him frequently to read to her. The Psalms of David had become her favorite. He settled into the chair beside her to read.

"Was Abram your birth father?" She opened the book to the page inscribed by his *gammi* and slid it toward him.

"*Ya.* Have I never told you?"

"*Nay*, never."

"He was a minister in the church before he died. He was also a cabinet maker. I thought of him often, as I . . . "

"As you what?"

"Well, the cabinets in your shop. They reminded me of his work. Anyway, he took his responsibility as a minister very seriously. *Mamm* and *Datt* Nafziger have his library of books on the church fathers. He studied our history and the persecution of our ancestors who fled to North America so that their children might live as *Gott's* Word instructed them. He believed each of us is responsible to know what *Gott* requires of us, and that knowledge requires that we study the Scriptures. The *Ordnung* guides us in community living; The Dordrecht Confession teaches us the foundation of our faith and doctrine. The Scripture feeds us and is the ultimate authority on all things. As our source of spiritual food, we need *Gott's* Word on a daily basis or else we grow weak, so he encouraged Bible reading. I guess he was a progressive minister; at least, he would be considered so nowadays. I do not know what was thought of him when he was alive."

"Do you remember him?"

"I have very few memories. *Mamm* and *Datt* Nafziger have kept his memory alive for me by sharing his books and teaching me why I am to read *Gott's* Word." Like most Amish, they rarely spoke of the dead, but *Mamm* never let him forget his heritage. "*Datt* Yoder wanted the church to grow beyond our communities in Ontario. He may never have imagined us here on the island, but his seed of hope for such a thing is what grew and brought us here."

Joel wondered if he'd said too much and made Lydia uncomfortable. She was fumbling at something on her writing desk; then she settled both hands in her lap. He wasn't sorry for sharing his story. No one other than his parents and Abe, named for *Datt* Yoder, knew. And no one ever spoke of it anymore.

He'd watched Lydia over the past several months as they prayed and read the Scriptures. Her spirit was lighter. Joel knew their Father in Heaven was at work healing whatever sorrows she carried too deeply to share with him. He hoped she would tell him someday, for her sake. Sometimes, silence became a filthy bandage, causing a wound to fester.

"I have something that belongs to you." Lydia was looking down into her lap. "I never meant to keep it so long. Anna found it when we were cleaning. I made her stop reading it. I just never had the courage to give it to you, and then I forgot." She lay a worn envelope on the table in front of him.

He recognized the envelope and handwriting immediately, like the hundreds he received from *Gammi* before she died.

Lydia's fingers trembled on the table. "I'll leave, so you can read it."

"Stay with me. I am not angry."

Lydia leaned back in her chair, and Joel opened the letter dated in the same month *Gammi* Yoder had died. As he read, she cautioned him to wait for marriage. She told him she believed in his dream. She asked him to pray for a troubled young neighbor who had lost her parents and sister. Joel stopped reading, as he began to comprehend the flow of the next sentences.

He raised his gaze away from the page and focused on the woman seated across from him. Beyond a shadow of a doubt, she was the one his gammi had described. He folded the letter back upon its worn creases. This was Lydia's story to share.

"You didn't read this?" He put the letter back in the envelope.

"*Nay.* Anna started to read it aloud, but I made her stop. I heard only enough to know coming to the island had been important to you for a long time. It helped me decide to say yes to our marriage. I didn't want you to miss your dream."

She'd never told him. How had he not known she'd been motivated out of concern for him? He'd thought he was rescuing her.

"I didn't finish reading this either. I think the rest of the story belongs to you. It's for you to tell me in your own time." Joel handed her the envelope.

He placed a kiss on her forehead and left before he changed his mind.

CHAPTER NINE

Lydia rose from the most restless night she could remember. Aware of Samy still blissfully sleeping in the same room, Lydia tiptoed down to the kitchen. A strong cup or two of *kaffi* was in order to face the eventful day ahead of her. The darkness was no bother, since she'd lain awake for the past hour. She could see well enough to stoke the fire and heat the water.

The stove was unexpectedly hot and a kettle already about to boil. "I've been awake. Thought I'd start it for you." Joel appeared as a dark figure in the doorway between the kitchen and living room.

So, he'd had trouble sleeping as well. Lydia didn't wonder at the reason. She'd lain in bed all night wondering how she could face him today.

Beulah Yoder's version of Lydia's story was a much kinder rendition than the one she must share. She almost wished he had read the letter and spared her the need to tell him. But then, his decision was the single most caring act she'd ever experienced with any man. And for the first time, she found herself wanting to share everything with him.

She could trust Joel. She knew that now.

He came beside her as she poured the hot liquid into two cups. "We can take it with us," he said.

She followed him outside, and he didn't require her to close her eyes again. The pitch black of the early morning hour ensured she could see nothing more than the spot ahead of them illuminated by his flashlight.

The light moved up to shine on a wooden post, then higher to reveal a perfectly painted sign with the words, Lydia's Amish Shoppe. Lydia's hand flew to her throat. How had she not known he was doing this?

"*Kumm*," Joel said. His hand slipped into hers. He'd held her hand the day before. Just as then, she was unable to refuse the comfort of his touch.

He opened the door and flipped on the light switch. The air buzzed as the large fluorescent lights warmed up. The electric lights absent from their home were allowed in barns and businesses. Slowly, the light increased until the interior became fully revealed. Lydia could hardly believe the sight.

"Am I dreaming?" She could easily be back in Lancaster, standing in the Yoder farmhouse and her own shop.

"Do you like it?" Joel's voice drew her eyes away from the room and back to his face, searching for her approval.

"*Ya*, Joel." Words couldn't do justice to his craftsmanship, to her astonishment, to her gratitude. "I am speechless."

"I wanted to surprise you." Joel pointed at the handmade chairs situated in front of a fireplace just the way she arranged them in Lancaster. "*Datt* wanted to help get the area ready—set up chairs and such—but I told him I'd take care of it. I wanted you to see it first. I wanted to show you before I move things for service today."

Her vision of the room blurred through her tears. "I don't know why I'm crying like a little *bobli*." Her voice wobbled. With the back of her hand, she wiped away the moisture from her eyes. "I'm really very happy."

He was always true to his word, this man who married her so she could escape the trap of her past. She found him faultless, with the exception of failing to tell her about Rachel. A mighty big exception, but how could she judge? She kept much bigger secrets of her own.

With every kindness from Joel, the weight of her past grew. She'd considered whether telling him everything would lighten the load. Where would she begin? How would she explain? A way to tell him eluded her. And so, she remained silent. She was convinced her silence hurt no one but herself.

Then came the letter, as if his grandmother watched from Heaven and intervened from the dead.

The truth will set you free. Her heart whispered to its pulsing beat.

She could feel the warmth of him in front of her, his breath caressing her forehead by his closeness, and she knew he was looking down at her. Waiting.

She looked up into the soft, brown eyes that always searched hers. His hands moved to her elbows, and his eyes drifted to her mouth. Could she resist a kiss, if that was his intent?

The truth will set you free.

The truth. *Ach,* she couldn't let him so close to her. He didn't know. And she couldn't tell the story now, before church, with so much to be done.

Regret swept over her for keeping him out when she wanted more than anything to let him in. But what about Rachel? And what would happen with Samy if Child Services knew her careless actions led to Louisa's death? Lydia knew what would happen. She couldn't bear the thought.

Joel stepped back, breaking the contact. "I've got a lot of work to do before the others begin to arrive." His voice sounded hoarse. His hands jammed in his pockets. "I best get to it."

Sabbath services brought together the eight families who belonged to their growing church district. Now that Bishop Nafziger's duties in Ontario had been taken over by a new bishop, he was to stay on the island. Regular meetings would resume every other Sunday. He also announced a new minister would be chosen by lot to serve under him, once their number grew to ten families.

Everyone already knew the way things would be done. Before the first couple left Ontario, the plans had been agreed upon by everyone—except Lydia, the only member from outside the original church. But no one knew who would serve as the next minister until the drawing of the lot revealed *Gott*'s will. On whom would the weight of responsibility fall?

Suddenly, Lydia's seat grew uncomfortable. She shifted, but the feeling worsened. She looked around to see who may be bothered with the mention of drawing the lot. In truth, she was the one plagued by her thoughts. *What if it were to be Joel?*

Joel was worthy—honest and fair—but *Gott* would not approve of Lydia as a minister's wife. The weight of her past failure felt like an ever-tightening knot around her neck. The further she got from it, the tighter it pulled.

Louise. Oh, sweet sister. I am so sorry. If only I hadn't listened. If only I had seen him for the scoundrel he was. I would never have left you. And you would never have left us.

If she allowed herself to dwell on the memory any longer, she would come undone. She turned her attention to the present and thoughts of how *Mamm* Nafziger was managing with Samy. All the other children sat with the women in church. Trained from infancy, even while still nursing, Amish children learned to sit quietly through the long service. *Mamm* Nafziger understood such an expectation was too high for little Samy and volunteered to watch her during the meeting.

Lydia wished her own sister had been afforded the same kindness. Louise was different from other children. No one named her ailment. Some called her simple. Others said she was spoiled. Her family knew neither was true. Louise was bright, sweet, and *goot*, although she rarely seemed in touch with the world around her. She had always been caught up in a world of her own making. Prone to wander. Prone to accidents. *Mamm* endured the whispers about the behavior without comment, but *Datt* grew bitter and withdrawn from the People.

Once again, Lydia found herself deeply grateful for the Nafzigers and their kindly ways. In some ways—not all—Samy reminded Lydia of her sister. Rather than judgment and impossible expectations, *Mamm* Nafziger offered Samy kindness and leniency.

Lydia stole a sideways glance at Joel. Was it possible he could give Lydia grace if she told him what happened that day? The reason she was unfit for motherhood.

His head turned. He'd caught her staring straight at him. His left cheek dimpled first; then a growing smile suggested he was no longer cross with her. Her spirits brightened, and she responded with a full smile of her own.

For a moment, she could have forgotten she was in the Sunday service, until the bishop's voice rose louder than the stir in her heart. Her cheeks burned as she quickly looked straightforward again.

If ever she had hoped for forgiveness and acceptance, today the longing was a hundred-fold stronger. She didn't need forgiveness for her sake alone. Joel deserved a real wife, and Samy needed a real family.

Joel's stomach was too tied up in knots to enjoy the luncheon in front of him.

He didn't even care if the bishop knew his mind had been anywhere but on the preaching that morning. They were decidedly settled on his wife. And *Datt* Nafziger undoubtedly knew that, too.

He was bound to get ribbed by the younger men for staring so blatantly at Lydia during the service. But no one could upset his joy in the knowledge Lydia had been looking straight back at him. He'd look a million times again to see the smile she'd given him.

That morning in the shop, he'd almost kissed her. But the look of fear that took hold in her eyes warned him to back off. He'd been rattled. Did she fear him? But that smile confirmed something else was the stumbling block between them.

Not knowing how to fix the problem was killing him.

His brother, Abe, sat beside him. Abe had no reservations about digging into his food-laden plate of cold cuts, pickled eggs, applesauce, and a giant mound of broccoli casserole. The latter proved the two of them weren't full-blooded kin. Broccoli and cheese together made Joel choke. The bishop was known to favor the combination, hence the over-abundant presence of all things broccoli and cheese at every church function. Abe was just as happy with the result as his *datt*.

The sight of Abe's shovel-sized bites did nothing to ease the disquiet in Joel's stomach. How long had it been since the man was last fed? Somehow, in the midst of a double-cheeked mouthful, Abe could also talk. "Sarah's been having pains." He chewed some more. "Baby's coming any day. She asked Rachel to come with her parents."

"Her sister, Rachel?" Joel asked.

"Who else?" Abe downed the last of his bite with a glass of apple cider. "Just thought you might like to know. They're coming."

"Why would I want to know?" Rachel was none of his concern anymore. Until Abe mentioned her, Joel couldn't remember the last time he'd thought of her.

Abe paused with a forkful of food hovering just outside his open mouth. "Older brother, you've never been good at understanding women. Now you're married, you have to wise up. That is, if you want Lydia to remain as cozy as she was last night." Abe closed his mouth around his food. He stabbed the fork in the air toward Joel and continued, "If memory serves me, you two haven't always been so close."

He meant their last night at Abe and Sarah's. Joel hadn't forgotten. He thought that issue had ended. He'd moved them out. Problem solved.

Until now.

Joel buried his head in his hands.

"I see you're coming to an understanding." Abe gulped his last swig of cider and headed to the dessert table.

Joel scanned the kitchen for Lydia. His *mamm* was washing up dishes already. Then he saw Lydia from the window headed to the barn with Samy. She wanted to see Amazon, no doubt. What a blessing the child was. He sensed she would somehow be the agent of healing in his odd, little family.

God had a purpose in bringing her to them, and Joel aimed to prove himself worthy of her. Not only for Lydia's approval, but for Samy's. He wanted her to know she deserved a father's love.

Joel excused himself to catch up to Lydia and Samy, but didn't find them in the barn. Through the wall, he heard Lydia's voice coming from the shop's side of the building. She was singing as she had the night before. Her voice was mellow and smooth. He wondered if she'd stop singing were he to enter. Leaning against the door, he listened and waited while enjoying each song she blended seamlessly into the next.

What a different kind of family we make.

And he didn't mind. In time, his family would be everything *Gott* intended for it to be.

Opening the shop door, he discovered Lydia in the rocker with Samy on her lap. Was she napping?

The sight stirred memories of first meeting her in his grandparents' farmhouse.

Was she happy here with him?

The little nest of red curls in the crook of her arm reminded him of the book cover she'd shown him one day as they packed up her belongings. She said it was about an orphan on the island. Maybe if he read the book, he'd learn what she expected when she chose to come here with him.

Lydia turned her head to the side to see him. "I think she needed some quiet." The words so simple, so motherly in explanation warmed his heart toward her again.

"I should leave."

"Not on our account." She motioned him to the other chair. "I've been telling her how this room reminds me of where I once lived.

Sometimes, we miss a place, but then a new place can start to feel like home."

He sat in the chair beside them and turned it sideways to see them. "Do you feel at home, Lydia? Here with me?" His heart began to beat too rapidly. Would she avoid giving an answer because she could not answer as he wished?

She stroked Samy's curls away from her temples. "I do feel at home." Her response came as soft as her touch to Samy's hair. "And I hope she will be as happy here as I am."

Her words thrilled him. His chest beat within him to a rhythm of hope. Then her eyes, green as sea foam, came up to meet his gaze, and he was undone.

"I will do all I can to make you both happy." How he wished he could take her in his arms. He wanted to wrap both of them close to him. The joy he felt was busting him open.

"I know you will. It's myself I am concerned about. I may not be a *goot mamm* for such a special child." A tear spilled over onto her cheek as she looked downward.

"You cannot be worried about that, Lydia. You are so naturally understanding of her. Look at her now, so peaceful in your lap. I saw what a handful she was becoming inside. You knew just what to do." He could go on, but her head was shaking in disagreement. He reached a hand to her knee. "Whatever is in the past is past. You never have to tell me if you do not wish. The woman you are now is what matters to me."

Her lips trembled. He wanted to pick up where he'd left her this morning and kiss her into knowing how he loved her. Instead, he waited for her to form the words hovering there.

"I want to tell you, Joel. I do not wish to have any secrets between us. The memories are just so painful to put into words."

A gust of air and the bang of the door flying open turned their attention. Abe stood just inside the room, his chest heaving with exertion. "There you are! We have to go. I have to get Sarah home. Can you get the midwife? She's an *Englisch* midwife. Lives in Cardigan. *Mamm* can tell you what to do." Abe left in as hasty a retreat as he had arrived.

How could he leave Lydia with such feelings? But the conversation could not be saved. Lydia was pushing him out the door right behind his brother.

CHAPTER TEN

The smell of freshly tilled earth had always excited Lydia. It held promises of flowers soon to come and the tastes of fresh vegetables from the garden. But today, she had little time to relax and enjoy the process. Chores simply must be done so that she and Joel could then go to see Sarah, Abe, and the new *bobli*. *Datt* Nafziger had brought them the news of the *bobli's* arrival early this morning, and they were giving everyone a chance to rest before they went to visit.

Lydia was still concerned about her neighbor, Cait. Whatever had happened to cause her to be unable to care for Samy had to be serious. If she got a chance, she would check on her neighbor before going to Abe and Sarah's, but she'd have to hurry and finish her work.

Joel had plowed her garden plot earlier as she hurried to do the Monday washing, which now hung on the line to dry. The red dirt crumbled through her fingers and back down to her newly planted row of snow peas.

A pull on her apron ties tugged her sideways. Beside her, Samy was no longer playing with the small spade and bucket that had been keeping her entertained. She was trying to go to Joel coming toward them from the fields. She'd be in a galloping run if she were not restrained by her own apron ties secured in a knot to Lydia's. How had the child managed that? Lydia had been somewhat amazed she hadn't wandered. She hadn't noticed their strings entwined as she hurried her to get the gardening finished while Samy was content at her side.

"*Ach*, Samy," Lydia said gently, as she untied the aprons and picked up the child. "What a *goot* little *maydel* you are! Was this your idea to help you stay close as I asked?" Even if the action was purely accidental, Lydia felt the praise was good for the child.

Joel reached them with a disapproving scowl on his face. "Did you tie her up?"

"*Nay!*" Did he think so poorly of her? "She did it herself. I think she wanted to be obedient and stay close."

Laughter erupted from Joel. "What a smart head you have, *liebling*. If only you could talk to us. The things you might say." He bent toward them and kissed Samy on the forehead. His eyes raised to look at Lydia. His look registered approval, but the sting of his accusation still burned in her heart. She looked away.

His hand rested on her shoulder, and she fought the temptation to shake it off. She didn't want to fight in front of Samy. She didn't want to fight at all. But to know that he would think so poorly of her was almost unbearable. Had she ever been unkind or cruel? Samy required supervision every second of the day, but she'd never tie her up.

His hand slid down to her elbow, and his voice pleaded, "Forgive me. I spoke before thinking, Lydia. Don't take it to heart." He held her hand. The sincerity in his eyes pled again. She nodded to this man who worked so hard to make a home for them and now for Samy.

"I understand." Yet her forgiveness of him did not change his opinion of her nor the pain of it.

Her heart had a mind of its own. If she could control it, she'd tell it to stop falling in love with a man who still loved another. But when Joel spoke to her in such a way with his touch warming her very soul, there was no more telling her heart what to do than ordering her newly planted lettuce and radish seeds to produce a crop of tomatoes.

Try all she might, nothing could remove the sadness in her heart that she would never be a mother. For even if Joel did not think badly of her, she was all too aware of her shortcomings. She was not unkind, nor was she cruel, but her negligence had been the cause of her sister's death. And for that, she could never forgive herself.

"Don't look so sad, my *fraw*." Joel tucked her stray hair back under her *kapp*. His skin was callused from hard work, yet his touch was tender and soft. "We've both accomplished a great deal already today. Let's eat lunch; then you can visit the Kings, as you wanted. The sun looks as if it will continue to shine, so I can even get a second field plowed by evening. All is well."

Lydia wished she could be so sure.

Grateful to Joel for minding Samy while she paid a visit to Mrs. King, Lydia stepped up to their neighbor's door. Lydia often visited the Kings. In the months after their first meeting, Lydia went to play with Samy, giving Cait a chance to get chores done unhindered. She and Cait had become as good friends as an Amish woman and *Englisch* neighbor could expect to be.

Over the past two days, since Samy had been brought to stay with Lydia and Joel, Lydia had been too hurried with Sabbath preparations to check on Cait. What could possibly have happened to cause Child Services to bring Samy to the Yoders? Uncertainty quivered in her stomach. *Please, Gott, let her be all right.*

No one answered her knock. Her unease grew. Should she peek into the garage to look for a car? *Ach,* this was one of those times a cell phone would be handy. She shrugged and walked around the garage to a side window. On tiptoe, she peeked inside, but the room was too dark to see anything. She squinted to no avail. Someone would take her for an intruder if she stood like this much longer.

The clunk of an engine and rattle of a lifting garage door startled her. Off balance, she turned quickly to face the road. Heat crept up her neck to her cheeks.

"Hello, Lydia." Cait called from her van window. "Go on in. I'll pull up behind you." Lydia heard the chuckle in her friend's voice and laughed at herself as well.

In the house, Cait laid her keys and purse on the kitchen counter. She pulled out her phone, swiped the screen, and let out a long breath before placing it down on the table. "The ride here has been the longest span of time that thing has remained silent since . . . Oh, you don't know, do you? Dan had a heart attack." She spoke the last words in a matter-of-fact tone, telling of how often she'd had to give the news. But the shock of them pushed Lydia back a step.

"I'm so sorry." Suddenly, Lydia's friend appeared older and more tired than she'd ever seen her. "Is he . . . How is he?"

"Dan's a fighter, you know. He woke up from surgery and said, 'Not gonna get rid of me that easy, ol' gal.'" A sad smile curved Cait's lips. "But it was way too close for my comfort. Way too close." The older woman swiped away a tear on her cheek. "Seeing you here is good medicine, though. Watching you jump when I opened the garage door was the first laugh I've had in days." Cait smiled wide with the memory.

"*Ya*, well, it's good to be of use for something," Lydia said and pulled Cait into a warm hug. "I was so worried after they brought Samy to us. I knew something terrible bad must have happened."

"All's well that ends well." Cait stepped out of the embrace. "Samy being with you is a good thing. And the good Lord is healing my Dan. He's a strong, old goat."

Relief washed over Lydia at the prognosis for Dan. Cait had to be way overdue for a rest and even a shower. How long had she been at the hospital? Lydia corralled her questions about Samy for another time. Her friend's needs came first.

Before she could offer help, Cait seemed to read her mind. "As you know, there's no place for Samy but a children's home. Dan's recovery is going to take weeks or months. Besides, we're just getting too old for a youngster like her. You and Joel are the answer to our prayers for that little girl." Fatigue drew Cait down to a chair as she spoke. "I expect you're the answer to the unspoken prayers of Samy's own heart."

Lydia hadn't allowed herself to think Samy may be with them on a permanent basis. They had been given no guarantee of adoption or even that the foster arrangement would be allowed to continue. Knowing she had no control over Samy's future frightened her. A war waged between her heart and mind, between fear and hope. "I don't know."

"What don't you know? She loves you and Joel and is never happier than when she is with you. I dare say, you're never happier either. And Joel dotes on her like she was his own."

"I don't think I can be what she deserves."

"Samy's most important needs are love, patience, and stability. You can give her all of those things. She will require speech therapy, but those things you take one step at a time. I'll be here to help you navigate through the red tape. She needs you, Lydia. You and Joel are her best hope."

The tops of Lydia's black shoes began to blur together from staring so hard at the floor. Cait's aged hand reached toward her, palm-side up. In a meek voice, she said, "Let's pray about it."

Lydia rested her own hand in her friend's open one. Cait's head bowed, and she began to pray. Lydia was unused to the custom of praying aloud together, yet she didn't want to offend her friend.

Where two or three are gathered together in my name, there am I in the midst of them.[3]

The Scripture flooded her mind, as it so often did since Joel began reading to her every day. A peaceful spirit settled in Lydia's heart. *Help me, Gott. If it be Your will for me to become a mother to Samy, I will. With my whole heart, I will. Help me not to fail her.* The silent cry of Lydia's heart ascended heavenward, as Cait's spoken prayer broke through Lydia's thoughts. "In Jesus' name, we pray. Amen."

A new confidence swelled within Lydia. She would do anything for Samy. For the first time, she began to believe she could.

She said goodbye with promises to stay in touch, as well as bring a home-cooked meal when Dan came home. Cait followed her to the end of the drive. Lydia knew she should leave so Cait could rest, yet her friend seemed unwilling to let her go.

With an expression filled with concern, Cait finally spoke her mind. "The most important thing you and Joel can do for Samy is to love each other."

As Lydia walked home, Cait's parting words echoed in her thoughts. Two-thirds of the way up the hill, she could see Joel's

---

3 Matthew 18:20, KJV

silhouette, tall and straight, close to the house. Closer to the top, Samy came into view with her arm stretched upward to hold Joel's hand. Joel waved. Lydia could imagine the smile too far away to come into focus.

Her heart snapped a picture.

Would Joel ever love her as a wife—a real wife? If she proved herself worthy to be a mother to Samy, then she could put the failure of her past behind her. And loving Joel would be so easy. So very easy. If only she deserved them both. If only Joel could love her in return.

Joel watched Lydia walking up the road from the Kings' house. His blunder that morning reminded him of the shaky ground on which their relationship stood. If he didn't need to talk to Lydia about Rachel, he'd be excited about visiting his brother and the new baby. But waiting until after Rachel arrived would be worse. He couldn't repeat the mistake of withholding from her again. If he dallied, Sarah would be the one to break the news of her sister's impending arrival. Joel groaned at the thought.

Gravel crunched behind him as a vehicle pulled into the drive. Two women got out of a blue sedan and headed toward the shop entrance.

"*Kumm*, Samy. We better see how we can help . . . "

What was he to call Lydia in this situation? She wasn't Samy's *mamm* or *aenti*; still, teaching Samy to call her Lydia didn't seem right. He'd ask Lydia.

Samy reached both arms upward to be carried. He swept her into his arms, overwhelmed by a protectiveness he'd never experienced.

"I wish we were your *mamm* and *datt*, little one." He pushed her hair away from her eyes. He knew she couldn't understand his dialect. How he wished she could talk to him. Suddenly, a longing to hear her sweet voice call his name took residence in his heart.

He had much to learn about the foster care system. From what the social worker explained, Samy was placed in their home as a temporary solution. None of them knew what the future would bring. But in his heart, Samy belonged here with him and Lydia. Would the church approve of adopting an *Englisch* child?

He was letting his feelings get ahead of himself. *Datt* Nafziger found making the decision as bishop to be unwise, since Joel was family. So, Samy's fate was to be determined by a meeting of the church elders in Ontario, not to mention the *Englisch* rules on the matter.

Nay, Joel knew better. Samy's future was in the hands of their Father in Heaven. Joel was doing good to manage one day at a time without taking on the work which belonged to *Gott* alone.

"You will always be loved here, Samy. Always. No matter what happens." This time he spoke to her in *Englisch*, hoping she understood every word.

At the top of the drive, he greeted the two customers as Lydia appeared not too far behind them. "My wife is coming. She runs the shop," he said to a middle-aged woman with dark hair. Behind her stood a teenager—her daughter, he supposed. "She hasn't opened yet, but she may give you a tour of the place."

The woman smiled back at him, and he went to meet Lydia at the end of the driveway.

She looked different somehow. He couldn't explain the change or the emotion that zipped through him as their eyes met. She'd never looked at him like this before. As though some partition between them had been removed, she felt closer—more present. Her slow smile caused his heart to somersault inside his beating chest.

Was it possible she might come to love him as he did her? In that moment, he dared hope he may one day earn her trust enough to express his true feelings to her.

His own mouth curved into what he hoped was a friendly smile but felt more like the expression of a schoolboy gazing at his first crush.

"The two women saw the sign and stopped. I told them you may be willing to show them around a bit." His words spewed out as fast as his heart thumped. Truly, he was acting like a schoolboy.

His traitorous memory recalled the warmth of her closeness on Saturday night as they played Dutch Blitz. She thought he was playing along because of Sarah. In truth, he'd relished every second of her nearness and dreamed of having her close again.

"*Danki.*" She took Samy and headed toward the waiting women.

"I have to finish some chores before we go to Abe's," he called after her, and she turned. "We can talk, then, about your visit. And I need to tell you some things."

"Of course." Lydia turned back to her customers, and soon, they all disappeared around the side of the building.

He had to talk to her about some things, all right. A discussion he was no more likely to enjoy than shoveling the manure.

CHAPTER ELEVEN

Joel's pitchfork hit the cement floor of the barn with a metallic scrape as he turned over fresh straw in Amazon's now clean stall. His teeth ground at the sound. He was behind and continued to hurry. Lydia and Samy had gone to the house already. He still required a good clean-up himself before going to see his newborn nephew.

A quick glance around assured him his tasks were complete. Then a long shadow stretched across the stall. Joel turned around to see *Datt* Nafziger standing in the doorway.

Joel leaned on the pitchfork and caught a few gulps of breath before tossing the pitchfork to the side. He stepped out the door beside the bishop and pulled it shut behind them. "I didn't expect to see you here. We're headed over to Abe's as soon I *redd* up."

"*Ya.* That's the business that brings me. Your *mamm* thinks maybe you ought to wait until tomorrow. Sarah's family all just arrived." No more explanation was necessary, but the bishop expounded anyway. "You're welcome anytime, of course. *Mamm* just thought tomorrow might be a better time after everyone has had a little rest."

"Of course, whatever *Mamm* thinks best." Joel was surprised at the disappointment he felt. The Erb family had traveled eighteen hundred kilometers. Joel lived a bare half-kilometer from his brother, and he'd be the last to see his own firstborn nephew. The mess was his own making, and he knew it. *Mamm* was trying to protect Lydia by not pushing the meeting of Abe's in-laws onto an already tiring day. "Have they named the *bobli?*"

Datt shook his head. "The delivery was long. We near lost them both. Sarah's terrible weak. And Abe . . . Well, I've never seen him so shaken." He paused and placed a hand on Joel's shoulder. The gesture usually imparted the man's strength but this time felt weary. "I expect we'll have a name soon enough, now that all is well."

"You're not going home alone, are you?" *Mamm* and *Datt* were renting a small house past the end of Annandale Road until their *dawdi haus* on Abe's property was completed. "You can stay here if Abe's place is too full." The thought of *Datt* Nafziger home without *Mamm* after such an ordeal didn't feel right.

"I'll think on it." *Datt* sounded almost convinced.

"Lydia will understand. You can help yourself to some of her fried pies." Joel attempted to sound cheerful despite the heaviness of the moment.

Datt Nafziger squeezed his hand still on Joel's shoulder. "*Danki, sohn.*"

Son. *Datt* Nafziger never had treated Joel as a step-child. Even in the early years of his marriage to Mamm when Joel was bitter over his father's death, Joel had treated his step-father with contempt; and still, *Datt* Nafziger had been patient and forgiving. A lump formed in Joel's throat. Could he be such a father to Samy, so he and Lydia could become a family for her?

Joel's opportunity for a moment alone with Lydia finally arrived after supper. *Datt* Nafziger retired early, not long after Lydia put Samy to bed.

Lydia dried the last supper dish, reached for a rag, and readied to wipe down the table. Joel put a hand out for the wet cloth. Her eyebrow raised in question, but she released the rag.

"Would you like to go for a walk? *Datt* will be here for Samy."

She nodded in agreement.

Joel began to wipe the table. "I'll do this while you get your shoes."

The smile she flashed at him as she slipped her feet into her shoes increased his anticipation ten-fold. "You are the most unusually helpful man I've seen around the house. And with Samy, too. *Danki*, Joel." She reached the doorway and looked back at him. "Aren't you coming with me?"

He tossed the dishrag into the sink. In two long strides, he was hovering over her in the doorway. "I thought you'd never ask," he teased, holding the door open for her.

After seven months of marriage, Lydia's heart still fluttered when Joel flirted. She tried to remember what she imagined life would bring when she agreed to a marriage of convenience. Truth was she hadn't thought this far ahead. How she ever imagined remaining satisfied as mere friends on a day after day basis with this man was a mystery. How the woman who held Joel's heart could turn away from his love was more mysterious.

"Which way?" Joel's question jerked her out of her wonderings. "Uphill means an easier walk back. Downhill means an easy walk now. Your call."

Lydia looked in both directions, then up at the stars. The night sky was clear. The moon was almost full. The above-average temperatures hugged her warmly while the scent of new grass and luscious pine enticed her toward the lesser-traveled natural path. "What if we walk through the fields instead?"

Joel looked down at her fabric sneakers. "It's soggy in spots."

"Consider me warned." She gave him a smile and tromped past him. With a look over her shoulder, she saw he was pleased.

She could flirt, too, although she hadn't much practice.

She'd always worried about leading a man on. She didn't want to give the impression she was interested in more than friendship. Not when she couldn't give an Amish man what he wanted—a wife and a mother to his children. But Joel married her expressly for the opposite reason. He didn't want to love her. He loved Rachel, whom he could not have.

The reality stung.

And yet, Joel said the past was past. She should try to offer him the same benefit. She shared this home with Joel. Not Rachel. A home in which she was free from the past, the gossip of everyone who refused to forget what she'd done. Joel gave her everything he thought would make her happy. And she would do her best to make him happy in return. She'd try to forget what she could not give. And what he did not want.

Joel caught up to her with ease. Weaving his fingers around hers, he tugged her in the direction of a grassy meadow he hadn't plowed. His hold remained firm, and she wondered how the act had become such a frequent occurrence. No matter the regularity, her heart still danced a little faster at his touch.

He mustn't feel it, she reasoned.

The swish of grass sounded to the pace of their feet. A bullfrog bellowed from the stream beyond the tree line. Joel began to hum. She recognized the hymn, *Whispering Hope*, as one of her favorites sung a cappella by a Mennonite choir back home.

Soft as the voice of an angel,
Breathing a lesson unheard.
Hope with a gentle persuasion
Whispers her comforting word.

The words began to slip unbidden from her tongue, and Joel blended his voice with hers in perfect harmony.

Wait till the darkness is over,
Wait till the tempest is done,
Hope for the sunshine tomorrow,
After the shower is gone.[4]

Their voices raised on the ending chorus, then ended simultaneously in silence. Joel was looking down at her. Far from any light, other than heaven's provisions, his expression was hidden. Her hand came up to touch his face to read what was written there. She paused halfway. She didn't dare. His arm wrapped around her waist and pulled her closer to him.

"I'd like a chance, Lydia. Let me prove myself to you." His smooth baritone voice had become hoarse.

A chance for what? Was he asking her to become his wife in the full sense? She willed her trembling legs not to flee. "I don't understand what you're asking." She braced herself for his response.

"To earn your trust and respect. To believe I will never betray you. And to be a good *datt* to Samy."

Somehow, her relief was not nearly as strong as the unexpected disappointment. She thought he at least meant to kiss her, but he was talking to her about Samy. She stepped back, thankful to the night for covering both her desire and embarrassment.

His mind was evidently on their mealtime discussion of Dan King's health and Samy's need for a permanent family.

"Don't run from me. I cannot bear when misunderstandings separate us. Why do you resist me?" The sadness of his voice made her regret turning away from him. She hadn't meant to hurt him.

---

4 Jim Reeves, "Whispering Hope," 1949.

"It's not you." Her legs felt weak. Lydia plopped to a sitting position on the ground. Wetness seeped through her dress. She didn't care. She couldn't stand, and there was nowhere else to sit.

Joel's shoes squeaked in the wet grass as he knelt beside her.

He moved into a squatting position. "We don't have to talk about it now," he said as he scooped her into his arms and stood up straight.

"What are you doing?" Lydia tried to jump down.

"You're weak, cold, and shivering. I'm taking you back to the house." Joel pulled her tighter to him. "You were easier to carry the time you were sound asleep."

"You can't carry me all the way back." Lydia glared but put her arms around his neck to keep from falling.

"Probably not." Yet, he showed no sign of slowing.

About a third of the way across the field, she felt the perspiration beading on the back of his neck. "Put me down, silly man. I can walk." He held her tighter and trudged onward. "Your pride is going to come before a fall, Joel Yoder."

He trudged onward, obviously too winded to respond.

"Okay, then, I see how it is. Put me down at the edge of the field. It's close enough to the house to save your manly pride."

She may as well have dared him to carry her all the way across the threshold. His heroics thrilled her, even as the absurdity became too hilarious to ignore. The more she tried to stop laughing, the harder her shoulders shook. Poor Joel. Why didn't he just put her down?

At the end of the field, she stopped laughing. "Joel, stop. You are going to hurt yourself."

He stared straight ahead. The house was so close. The yard was level. "I can't quit now."

When they reached the porch, he tripped on the top step, sending them both sprawling. His hand flew out to stop their fall just inches from crushing Lydia underneath him. He fell over onto his side and inhaled great gulps of air. After a few good breaths, he rolled his head to the side to see if Lydia was all right. She pinned him with an I-told-you-so gaze before a smile curved her lips upward.

The squeaky hinge of the front door sounded.

Great. They'd woken *Datt* from his much-needed sleep.

But the shadow that crossed them was feminine. Lydia looked up at a woman who appeared to be a softer version of Sarah Yoder. She hadn't known her sister-in-law had a twin, but more than a mere family likeness gave away the woman's identity. She expected to meet Rachel when they visited Abe and Sarah to see their *bobli*. Even though Joel hadn't mentioned her coming with the family, she'd prepared herself. Her wildest imagination hadn't planned for an introduction in this state—wet, disheveled, and flat on her back, lying next to Joel.

Lydia jumped to her feet fast enough to feel dizzy. She dug her toes into the soles of her shoes and willed herself to stop spinning.

Joel still lay on the porch staring at Lydia. Of all things. If she could pull herself together, why couldn't he?

She turned away from his gaze and felt her hair drop first to her shoulders and then down the length of her back. Instinctively, her hand flew to her head. Her prayer *kapp*? She looked at Joel again to see the *kapp* lying in his lap.

Rachel's face flooded to a deep shade of crimson, and Lydia knew she'd seen the same sight. Rachel looked away from them both and emitted a piteous squeak. "Salome sent me with food for the bishop. She thought he was home alone. I saw his buggy here. I didn't mean to

. . . to . . . " Muttering an incoherent apology, the raven-haired beauty descended the same stair over which Lydia and Joel had tripped just moments before.

The trot of a horse attached to a small, two-wheeled cart was barely beyond the driveway and headed back toward Abe's place when Joel burst into uproarious laughter.

"Joel Yoder!" Lydia's voice sounded stern even in her own ears, except she'd read the mischief on his face lying there with her *kapp*. She couldn't help but take pity on the woman. "Is that how you think a man ought to treat a woman he loves?" *Ach*, love was not the word she meant to use—aloud. "I mean, a woman who is our guest." The attempt to backtrack fell flat.

The bewilderment on Joel's face flickered into sadness before stalling on frustration. "I don't know, Lydia Yoder." He emphasized her surname. "If you can tell me how the woman I love wishes to be treated, I'll be happy to oblige. But I don't think she knows what she wants yet." He stormed to the barn, leaving Lydia in his wake, swirling in a cloud of confusion.

CHAPTER TWELVE

Lydia bit down on her ink pen. If only Mary were here. Her brother's wife had been her confidant since childhood, but Mary had no more free time for a visit to Prince Edward Island than Lydia had to go to Lancaster. Mary always saw straight to the heart of the matter when Lydia saw only fog and shadows.

Lydia rifled through a stack of letters from Mary, desperate for any clues her intuition may have left about Joel.

Nothing.

Joel's behavior the previous evening made no sense. He acted as if Rachel were a pesky sister to tease, not a woman he wished he'd married. She was almost afraid to interpret his comments as he stormed off to the barn and far too unsure to believe what she thought he had implied. Lydia would have to ask outright for Mary's opinion in the letter she was writing.

"I'll be ready in a minute," Joel called from downstairs.

She'd have to finish the letter after they returned from Abe's.

With Samy in tow, Lydia settled into the buggy beside Joel. She wasn't prepared to face Rachel Erb so soon after the previous night's fiasco. Apparently, moving to another country hadn't resolved all her headaches and included new ones.

"I'd like to finish our conversation from last night." Joel's attention remained on the road as he spoke. "*Datt* agreed to come watch Samy, so I can take you to dinner. He misses his grandchildren in Ontario. I think it's hard for a man his age to make such a big change."

"But he sees you and Abe."

"*Ya*. He does." Joel shot her a brief glance. "Would you like to go to dinner?"

"It's very thoughtful of you."

"But you're not wishing to go." His tone was flat. She'd clearly disappointed him somehow with her response.

She hadn't understood she had a choice. Was he inviting her—as though he were courting her? "*Ya*, I want to go. Very much."

The released tension in his arms slackened the reins. Amazon responded in a trot, speeding Lydia to the inevitable meeting with the Erb family.

Standing in Sarah's kitchen, the contrast between this day and the last one Lydia had spent in the same place was remarkably different. Today, the stirring hope a new life brings to a family filled Abe and Sarah's home. The birth of each of her nieces and nephews brought this same joy to her brother's home. An ache stabbed at her heart from the knowledge her home with Joel would never see a day like this.

Give it to Me. A whisper from her spirit implored. Did she have the courage to hope *Gott* might forgive her?

Turning toward a sound from behind her, she saw Joel standing in the doorway. His broad shoulders leaned against the framework. Heat flooded her face at his clear admiration of her from a distance. How long had he been there?

"Are you ready to meet Samuel?" He held out his hand to her. "They named him after *Datt*. And if I'm not mistaken, Samuel the *bobli* will soon lead Samuel the bishop around by the nose."

Lydia followed Joel to the living room. A few minutes later, Sarah returned from her room, where she had gone to change Samuel's diaper. She moved to Lydia and Joel and held out her son to them. A tap on Lydia's elbow prodded her forward.

Sarah smiled at her—a novel experience. Fatigue shadowed her sister-in-law's eyes, while pure joy reflected in her voice. "Samuel, meet Uncle Joel and *Aenti* Lydia."

The *bobli* was beautiful and round enough to leave no guess as to the cause of his petite mother's arduous labor. His eyes shut, and his tiny lips slacked with sleep. Sarah nestled the warm bundle wrapped in blue into the crook of Lydia's arm. Careful not to wake him, she brushed his soft cheeks.

Joel peered over her shoulder to see his nephew. "Who do you think he looks like?"

"Not his uncle, I'm sorry to inform you," Lydia teased.

"I agree. He's Abe all over again," Sarah said as she took a seat by her husband.

"If you wish for a child like you, Joel," all eyes shifted to the bishop on the far side of the room, "then you know what to do."

What in the world? Lydia had never heard a bishop speak of such private affairs between a married man and his *fraw*.

"*Ya, Datt.*" Joel broke the quiet with a nervous laugh. "You have a point."

Mamm gave Lydia a sympathetic nod and reached out for the *bobli*.

The bishop still had Joel pinned with a probing stare and lifted brow. He appeared far from remorseful for his comment.

Ach, poor Joel.

Lydia slipped her arm around Joel's, raised on her toes, and touched her lips to his temple. The problem with spontaneity was the absence of a plan for the aftermath. Her heels thudded back down to the floor and begged to run away, but Joel latched onto her sleeve.

"If *Gott* be willing, *Datt,* you will have grandchildren enough to farm all of Prince Edward Island. For now, I have a date with my *fraw* for dinner in Cardigan."

"A date? That's for courting. What use do married men and women have for a date? That's an *Englisch* tradition." Sarah's *mamm* clicked her tongue. The apple didn't fall far from the tree in their family. But Sarah said nothing.

The bishop turned to his wife. "I approved. Gives us time with little Samy." An unspoken understanding passed between the bishop and his wife. *Mamm's* brows rose in a whatever-it-takes expression.

"Well, then, don't let us keep you." *Mamm* Nafziger rose from her chair to see them out the door. "Cardigan is such a long drive. Joel, you must arrange for a taxi driver. And Lydia, don't you worry about Samy. We'll take care of everything."

Sarah's *mamm,* Belinda Erb, met them in the hallway. "You're not leaving already?" The relief in her voice was obvious. Lydia noticed Rachel had made herself scarce and pitied her once more.

"They'll be back. I'm sure you will get to visit sometime soon," *Mamm* Nafziger called over her shoulder, all the while shooing Lydia and Joel through the kitchen and onto the porch.

Joel paid the cab driver for the fifteen-mile ride to the harbor village of Cardigan and asked him to return in a couple hours. With time to spare before dinner, Joel had stopped the cab by the wharf to explore the area with Lydia on foot. Joel hadn't come for the food, anyway. He'd never cared for restaurants. He only wanted Lydia to know he appreciated her. And so much more.

After the previous night, he figured she still misunderstood his affections for Rachel. He'd like to set the record straight. He also wasn't satisfied with pretend affection in front of his family. Each time he enjoyed the attention, his conscience pricked him. How had he considered living a lie to be a wise choice?

He hadn't. He'd believed love would grow between them.

Would it? Each day brought him to a different conclusion about Lydia's feelings.

"They know, don't they?" Lydia stood still at the edge of a stairway leading to the water.

He wished he could pretend not to understand the question. "Sure sounded that way."

"I feel as guilty as if I'd lied to them."

"So do I."

She kept walking. He hung behind several steps. The water lapped against the concrete wharf. The clear sky reflected as broken shards of light across the inlet to the opposite side of the harbor. Small boats sat empty at anchor. Except for an occasional car crossing the Wharf Road Bridge, Joel and Lydia were alone. Joel sat down on a bench a few feet from where Lydia stood by the seaside.

She turned around to face him. "If you want to tell them, I understand. I will be embarrassed, but to lie is a sin."

What he wanted was for her to love him. She was strong and kind with equal measure. She fought for others. And she won. At the auction. With Samy.

She was remarkable. Joel had never admired Rachel, or any other woman, as he did Lydia.

"I won't tell them there's no hope for us, Lydia. As long as we're making an effort, there's no lie. Will you give us a chance?"

A gentle breeze whirled her dress around her legs. She hugged her arms around her waist and looked back to the sea.

At the very moment he could no longer resist going to her, she came to sit beside him.

How did he expect to unlock the secrets of her heart without transparency of his own?

"Lydia." She faced him as he hoped she would. He brushed at the errant wisp of hair, which always escaped her prayer *kapp*. "I am not in love with Rachel. I will never break my vow to you."

Her eyes were wide. He held her gaze, willing her to believe him.

She looked down at her lap and drew a deep breath as though for courage to speak. "I loved a man who took a great deal from me. So much. And then, he abandoned me for another woman."

Joel had often wondered whether a man was the cause of Lydia's fear of marriage. Her confirmation stoked a fire inside him. "Was he Amish?" Joel hoped not, even as he asked.

"*Ya.*"

Joel watched Lydia's eyes pool with unshed tears. How was a non-violent man to curb his wish for revenge on whoever hurt her? *Dear Gott, help me control my anger against this man. Grant me the wisdom to understand what has happened to Lydia, and how to help her heal.*

Just then, Lydia's hand rested on his knee, her eyes full of sincerity, and all his anger fled. In the moment, no one else mattered. Only he and Lydia existed. "You deserve a chance, Joel. I will try to give us a chance, too." And he knew she would. Everything Lydia did, she did with her whole heart.

"It's enough for now, Lydia. More than enough."

He had been so blind to the pain his silence regarding Rachel had caused Lydia. To think she'd done all the work of a *fraw* for him and worked so hard in their home without complaint while believing she'd been relegated to second-best again. Joel couldn't fathom such faithfulness.

"I'm sorry, Lydia. Sorry I let you wonder about Rachel for so long. Sorry I am such a *dumm-kobb*."

Her head rested against his shoulder. In the quietness, he hoped they both found a measure of peace.

"Joel." Lydia's voice was barely louder than a whisper. "I need to tell you the rest of the story."

"All right. I will listen."

She moved, not far, only enough to break the contact between them. Her gaze stretched far beyond the horizon as she began. "I had a little sister. Her name was Louise. She was like Samy in many ways. The people were not as patient with her differences as your family has been with Samy. Simeon, Hiram Glick's brother, was my beau. I was only sixteen. He was nineteen. At first, he was nice, but slowly he became possessive of me and my time. Then he began to mock Louise and made me feel guilty for the time I spent with her. Instead of breaking off our courtship, I tried harder to please him. I enjoyed his ways of making me feel like a woman." A scarlet blush colored her cheeks, and she paused.

"I cannot judge you for that, Lydia." *Nay*, he'd laid his own mistakes at the foot of the cross to be remembered no more. Lydia deserved as much. Someday, he may even be able to pray for Simeon, though not today. Pushing aside his anger at the man, Joel enclosed Lydia's soft hand in his own and waited for her to continue.

"I made excuses in my mind for how he treated Louise. I even ignored his flirtation with other girls. He made me feel foolish if I confronted him. I should have talked to my *mamm*, but her worries over *Datt's* illness and Louise's condition kept me from troubling her. Mary and Ben were just married. She would have listened, but I thought I could handle things on my own."

Joel watched as Lydia twisted uncomfortably beside him. He wished he could say she didn't need to finish, but he knew she had to be free of the burden. He moved his arm back around her for comfort.

She leaned against him for a short moment, then pushed back far enough to look up at him. "Oh, Joel, I despise myself for what I must tell you."

"Lydia, you cannot. You must not despise yourself when *Gott* Himself has shown such love for you." Joel's heart could scarcely beat for the heaviness of the weight he felt for Lydia.

"You don't understand. Louise was hit by a car. She died because I had run off with Simeon to enjoy his kisses when I should have been watching her."

Joel held his sobbing *fraw* and pressed her into his chest as her pain fractured his own heart into pieces.

"Lydia." Joel stroked her hair as he spoke, "I'm sorry for what happened. Sorry for the pain Simeon caused. Sorry for the guilt you carry. But you have to know, I would never change my mind about you. There's nothing I want more than you here with me."

In Joel's arms, Lydia might believe anything was possible. Maybe *Gott* was giving her a second chance with Samy and Joel to redeem herself. She wouldn't fail them as she had Louise.

Give it to Me. The heart whisper called to her again. Lydia pushed it back. Redemption couldn't be so simple.

How could she ever forget the agony on her *mamm's* face or the brokenness in her voice? "Lydia, I trusted you." The words had sliced through Lydia's heart. She'd wondered how *Mamm* knew what she and Simeon had done. Shame and confusion enveloped her in a dirty blanket. She wanted to wash herself free of Simeon's touch. But *Mamm* knew nothing of her struggle in the woods. She was mourning a different loss. And all too soon, Louise's broken form came into view, along with the police officers standing in their house questioning Ben and their *datt*.

Louise had been playing in the ditch by the mailbox when a drunk driver came down the road. The officers called Louise's death an accident. They would charge the driver with manslaughter, regardless of her parents' wishes. Only Lydia knew her *mamm* was right. Louise's death was Lydia's fault. Everything was her fault. Even as the police left the Miller home without a single allegation directed at her, grief had held Lydia captive as her own guilt suffocated her.

Nay, redemption was not for someone like her. And yet, beside her sat a man who forgave her without a second thought. Though she'd been taught her whole life the way of her faith was to forgive, she'd rarely experienced the type of acceptance Joel offered. Was *Gott* offering the same to her?

"*Kumm.*" Joel took her hand and stood. "A walk will help clear your thoughts."

Joel led her on a long stroll through the small village. His hand in hers promised he was not turning away from her. She didn't deserve a man like Joel.

They crested a hill and walked through a public park. The longer they went, the more Lydia felt her mind and heart clear. Telling Joel about Simeon and Louise was the hardest thing she recalled ever doing. She never thought she'd find the words or the courage. Now that she'd finally told him, she realized thoughts of the past didn't bear the same sting.

"There's a public washroom. Would you like to *redd up* before we head to the restaurant? I mean, you look fine. Beautiful. I just meant . . . "

"I know what you mean. I will be right back." Lydia tried not to laugh at his blundering. He was cute when he didn't know what to say. Suddenly, she was very much looking forward to their dinner date.

At the restaurant, a friendly waitress seated them near a large fireplace. A giant, wood-carved clipper stared down at them from the mantel. Lobster was the favorite local fare, but Lydia felt more at home ordering the hot turkey sandwich with peas and whipped potatoes. The plate came doused in gravy. No one ought to complain about the portions. The double-decker sandwich was enough for two.

Joel bent his head over his plate piled with strips of sirloin smothered in onions. She waited for him to inhale and declare it must be *goot*. He always did, even when she'd burned his favorite casserole.

"Smells *goot*. Must be *goot*." Joel declared his approval and bowed his head for silent prayer. His hand slipped over hers under the table and rested on her knee, leaving her too *fahuddeld* to pray. In all the times he'd held her hand in prayer, she'd never experienced the shock of warmth that flooded through her this time from his touch.

"*Vass is letz?*" Joel whispered. She looked up at him with fork in hand, waiting for her to begin. His upturned lips indicated he was amused. He must think she was a silly *maydel*.

Heat flooded her face. "Nothing." She plunged her fork into the enormous concoction of turkey, bread, and gravy in front of her. *Nothing but my heart healing because of you.*

Joel cleaned his plate and pushed his chair back for breathing room. "I feel like the glutton I am because I fully intend to top this off with one of your sweet pies at home."

Lydia laughed at him and pointed to her own plate. She'd eaten two-thirds, and another bite would split her wide open. "I don't see how you do it."

"You won't be laughing when I'm a fat, old man because of your pies." He gave her a sobering stare, followed by a wink.

"Don't blame me, Joel Yoder. It doesn't matter a jot who makes the treats; you gobble them up." Lydia picked up her water glass and sipped on it, as though she'd had the final word.

The smile he gave her warmed her straight down to her toes. "Desserts maybe. Some things I want from only you, Lydia."

The water she swallowed strangled her. Her cough was met by a firm hand thrust into her back. "Are you okay, Lydia?"

Lydia shook her head and managed to look up to the feminine voice of her rescuer—Traci Holbrook, Samy's social worker.

Joel stood and shook her hand. She was introducing a man who appeared close to her age and wore a business suit. Lydia managed to stand. The man, introduced as Carl Talbert, held up a hand. "Please don't get up. We didn't mean to interrupt."

"We're happy to see you." Joel amazed Lydia at his smooth transition between Amish farmer and the *Englisch* world. If not for his clothing, Carl Talbert would have been hard-pressed to peg Joel as an Amish man. Joel directed his attention to Mr. Talbert. "We are grateful to Traci for all she does for us and Samy."

"Thank you." Traci bit her lower lip and moved toward another table.

Mr. Talbert followed, asking in a voice loud enough to be heard, "They're clients? You have Amish caring for other children? Non-Amish children? How does that work?"

"Everything has been done legally and in order, even by your standards." Traci's voice carried across the two tables separating them.

"If not, you better believe I'll find out. The last thing we need is Amish farmers using foster kids as a labor force."

"Don't be rude," Traci hissed at the man before sending Lydia an apologetic look over her shoulder.

Lydia turned so no one could see her face, except Joel. She'd wondered what the Amish would say if she and Joel continued caring for Samy. Why hadn't she considered what the *Englisch* might say? Traci had almost begged them to take Samy. Cait and Dan King had both expressed support and encouragement. None of their other neighbors complained. Were they merely polite, or did others feel like this man?

"Are you ready to go?" Joel asked with eyes full of concern. He must have the same questions.

Lydia nodded. "More than ready."

CHAPTER THIRTEEN

Mid-September

"La-la?" Samy's call for Lydia rang through the shop. *Mamm* Nafziger had taken Samy to see their new *dawdi haus*, as well as a litter of newborn kittens. Lydia used the free time for an inventory of the shop.

"Over here," Lydia called to them.

The sound of small, quick steps came toward her, bringing a joyful Samy. "Ook, La-la." Her hands flew over her head with a sheet of paper gripped between them. Random streaks and splotches of watercolor bled together across the page held up like a masterpiece.

"I see. Is it kittens?"

Samy shook her head sideways. "Yo-yo." To Samy, Joel was Yo-yo.

Lydia leaned closer and inspected the picture. "I see now. It's Joel."

Mamm Nafziger joined them. "She has been a very *goot* girl today," she said making Samy beam brighter. "We even made oatmeal cookies. I brought her a treat for after dinner." The brown bag she handed Lydia felt as though it held enough treats for a week.

"*Danki, Mamm*." Lydia then prodded Samy, "Did you say thank you?"

Samy pressed the palm-side of her fingers against her lips, then motioned her hand away from her face in the sign for thanks.

"That's right. Now, can you say the word?" Lydia followed instructions from Samy's speech therapist to encourage spoken language. The months of therapy made a night-and-day difference in Samy.

"Ta." Samy replied, then slipped through the aisles to the toy chest kept just for her. Old pots and pans rattled as she re-played cookie-making from her time with Salome.

A smile turned *Mamm* Nafziger's mouth upward, and the approval warmed Lydia's heart. Joel, Samy, and Lydia were anything but a traditional Amish family. And yet, over the months since Samy came to live with them, they had grown together as though they were always meant to be a family.

"Lydia?" *Mamm* Nafziger's voice was gentle as usual. "The bishop has a special request for you. Autumn will bring new families to our community with more school-age children. We cannot afford a teacher until more families come. The mothers teaching at home will need supplies."

"I'm pleased to carry school books and any other necessities. I won't even charge at a profit for the school materials."

"We hoped you might help guide the women folk, since you were a teacher."

Ideas spun through Lydia's head. In the past, an Amish publisher in Ontario had been helpful in answering her schooling inquiries—even sent a catalogue.

"*Ya.* It's a *goot* idea. I'll speak to Joel about it."

"The bishop will be glad to hear it." *Mamm* fidgeted with her apron, then spoke in a lower voice. "I was wondering. Could we go to the house and talk over *kaffi?*"

Once Lydia laid Samy down for a nap, she joined *Mamm* in the kitchen. *Mamm* had already prepared two cups of steaming *kaffi*. Lydia uncovered the fresh oatmeal cookies and set them on the table.

The drink was too hot to sip, so Lydia dunked a cookie. "These are delicious."

Lydia devoured another cookie and waited to hear *Mamm's* real reason for wanting to talk, which was likely nothing to do with teaching or homeschool.

Mamm dried her hands and sat in front of Lydia. "Joel looks like his *Datt* Yoder. You would've guessed as much, since he resembles me very little." *Mamm* opened her mouth as if to speak more, then sipped from her mug instead.

Lydia tried to conjure an image of the older woman before her hair turned the current white and gray. Did Joel's thick, black hair come from his father? His height must have. *Mamm* Nafziger was shoulder-height to Lydia.

"He has Yoder looks and mannerisms, for sure. But *Datt* Nafziger has been his role model. Watching my children grow into adults, I realize how much we've taught them by example. Some lessons *goot*. Others not so much." Sadness crossed her features.

Lydia reached out a hand. "You've done a *wunderbaar goot* job, *Mamm*."

Lydia meant to be a comfort, but *Mamm* shook her head. "*Nay*, Lydia. *Gott* has been gracious to protect my children from my many mistakes, especially Joel. When Abram died, his best friend offered to marry me. I agreed to the marriage to provide for Joel." *Mamm* turned to look over her shoulder through the kitchen window, either searching for Joel or lost in the past. "Samuel and I never spoke to the children of that first year. Whether he understood or not, Joel was there. I believe he waited so long to marry because of it. And now, he expects . . . "

Lydia could finish the moral for her. Joel expected a happy ending to his own marriage of convenience.

"Sometimes, we have to let go of the past, so we can experience the future." *Mamm's* voice pulled Lydia's eyes up to the older woman's filled with compassion.

Lydia didn't understand. How could she just move on as though her sin and failure held no consequence?

Give it to Me. The heart whisper called to her spirit again.

Lydia set down her mug. Her finger splayed against the wood grain of the table top beside it. "I don't know how."

The soft flesh of *Mamm's* hand lay on top of Lydia's. "*Gott's* forgiveness is a free gift because His Son already paid the price of all our sins. All you must do is accept it."

"How can you be so sure?"

"Because His Word tells me so. There is no forgiveness without faith, *liebling*. Go to the Scripture. Pray for faith, and He will show you. He is the Rewarder of all who diligently seek Him."

Joel waved to his *mamm* as she rode past in her buggy. Now that planting season had ended and harvest was near, the farm required his attention from sunup to sundown. He was glad of the relationship between Lydia and *Mamm*. She received letters from both Anna and Mary back in Lancaster, but she needed friends here.

Cait King was another woman for whom he was grateful. He'd paid a visit to Dan King and offered to put up his field of hay. Their neighbor was still weak but happy to be home from the rehabilitation center. His appreciation for Joel's offer was reward enough for the small favor. Joel's baler would make quick work of the small field.

Joel stopped the tractor when he saw Cait standing at the edge of the field.

He'd hoped for an opportunity to speak to Cait. He'd tried to forget the comment made by Traci Holbrook's friend at the restaurant, but a decision regarding Samy continued to be delayed.

"Hello, Cait."

"Hello. I saw you at work and thought I'd thank you for your visit to Dan. You lifted his spirits."

"I'm glad to hear it." Joel hopped down to talk. "I have a question. I'm not sure who else to ask."

Cait nodded.

"A few months ago, I took Lydia to Cardigan for dinner. We bumped into Traci Holbrook, the social worker."

"Yes, I know Traci."

"The man with her voiced concerns about Samy living in an Amish home. I wouldn't say anything, except we still have no decision regarding her adoption. I realize these things take time, but this man spoke as though he had some authority. He sounded none too pleased about an Amish couple taking in a non-Amish child."

A shadow crossed Cait's face before she replaced it with her usual calm. "What was his name?"

"Carl Talbert. If others share his opinion, could there be a problem?"

"Potentially." Cait was direct as always. "We've had our hearts broken many times through the years. But everyone has opinions, Joel, and most are just that—simple opinions. You cannot worry over everything you hear."

"I suppose you're right. I'll have to stop letting it nag me. I fear for Lydia, most of all." He didn't want to betray Lydia by expounding, but he feared her new spiritual growth would suffer a severe setback were they refused allowance to adopt. "*Danki,* Cait."

Joel walked toward the tractor. Would Lydia's heart bear the disappointment if Samy were taken from her?

"Joel." Cait called his attention back to her. "Samy has no parents or family with any rights to her. I believe the courts would be open to adoption when they see she is loved and well cared for. As long as Samy is not being forced to become Amish, it's unlikely the courts would object." She motioned him back toward her. "I'm no lawyer, but I can recommend a good one. In fact, I'll give you his number."

Despite striving daily to live a simple, *Gott*-pleasing life, difficult choices invaded like thistles in a hay field. Joel placed the sticky note with a lawyer's name and phone number into his pocket. He prayed he'd never have to make contact.

"Thank you, Cait, for your honest advice."

With a heavier heart, Joel returned to his task of cutting hay. He sensed Samy's future rested upon decisions made far beyond his or Lydia's reach. The courts were one obstacle. The reputation of the People was also a consideration. They must shine the light of Christ to the community. When the *Englisch* world and Amish world mixed, the choices became more difficult.

Until now, the people considered caring for Samy as an act of Christian charity. If a legal fight became necessary, members of the congregation may view the process as a threat to their life of separation from the outside world.

Joel wished for more time to spend with Lydia. He'd had little time to court her with the summer months so full of farm work. Marriage before courtship was a backwards way to go about things.

He needed to win Lydia's affection, or their marriage would remain a mere partnership.

Their friendship was a solid foundation. But who laid a foundation and never built the house? Not Joel.

He parked near the barn, then headed to the house for a sneak visit with his *fraw*.

Inside, he removed his mud-caked boots. He was covered in dirt up to his knees and elbows. The small washroom off the kitchen was where Lydia preferred for him to clean up. Careful not to leave a mess in the area of the gas-powered washer, he reached for a clean pair of pants and headed to the utility sink on the opposite side of the room. Lathered and scrubbed up to his biceps, Joel rinsed the grime down the drain and grabbed a towel.

"*Danki*." Lydia's voice startled him. She stood just beyond the door. How long had she been there?

"For what?"

"Being clean." She motioned to the towel and his clean trousers. "And quiet. I'm letting Samy sleep until the speech therapist arrives."

"She does do better after a nap." Joel had witnessed the difference himself.

Lydia came into the room. Her expression indicated he'd done more to please her than *redd up* after plowing. "Some men wouldn't notice about a child's naps or moods."

She took his towel. He supposed to toss it in the dirty clothes bin. Instead, she leaned up on her toes and wiped his forehead. She looked at the smudge mark on the cloth and gave him a sideways grin. His heart thudded against his chest. She raised her hand again. On impulse, he caught her wrist and pulled her closer.

He'd promised himself to make their first kiss romantic. What a fancy notion. He was a plain man in need of a kiss from his beautiful *fraw*. Lydia relaxed her arm. Her eyes searched his without fear or hesitation. After all these months, was she finally ready?

He bowed his face toward her, and she responded by tilting her own upward to him. "Lydia . . ."

"Yo-yo!"

Lydia jerked away.

"Yo-yo." A waving hand and flapping paper begged for his attention. "She painted a picture at *Mamm* Nafziger's this morning." Lydia looked amused. "It's you."

Joel bent down to look at the picture. "Thank you." He used *Englisch* as the therapist requested. "*Gammi* showed you how to use all her pretty colors, didn't she?" His *mamm* painted landscapes. She'd even sold them for a substantial amount back in Ontario.

Samy nodded.

"I like it very much."

She beamed and ran off to play.

"I'm glad you didn't scold her for drawing your image."

"*Nay*, we cannot make her Amish." Joel studied Lydia's expression. She'd misunderstood. "I wouldn't break the child's spirit, regardless, but it's something Cait said to me today."

"Why would Cait say something?"

"I asked her about that man, Carl Talbert. I know I shouldn't let his comments bother me, but I wanted her opinion."

Lydia nodded understanding. "And?"

"She feels as long as we don't force Amish ways on Samy, then there will be no trouble." Should he mention her suggestion about the lawyer?

He felt the softness of her cheek under his fingertips as he brushed her hair back under her *kapp*. She looked up at him as though he released her from a great worry.

She stood on tiptoe and kissed his cheek and scooted out the door after Samy. "Meredith will be here soon," she called over her shoulder. Joel marveled at how far they'd come. Yet they had so far to go.

"Welcome, Meredith." Lydia opened the door for the speech therapist. Petite, athletic, and well-tanned, Meredith arrived smiling and full of energy twice a week for an hour-long session with Samy. Sometimes, Lydia was asked to observe and learn with Samy. Most often, Lydia was to remain unseen, enabling Samy to focus her attention on the therapy.

Meredith handed Lydia a manila envelope. "I collected information on Autism Spectrum Disorder and sensory dysfunction. You understand, I cannot diagnose Samy; but as a speech pathologist, I have a great deal of experience with children with autism."

Lydia nodded. Samy would have to see a specialist for a diagnosis. However, the combined experience of Cait, Traci, and Meredith pointed to the same conclusion—Samy had autism. They called it a spectrum and believed she was on the high-functioning end of the scale.

"I believe this information will help you navigate through your experience with her. Children with special needs require guardians who are informed well enough to advocate on their behalf. I hope this is helpful."

"Thank you. We want to do all we can for her." Lydia opened the unsealed envelope and pulled out a brochure.

"I noticed you sell books in your shop, so I also printed a list of helpful resources. I assumed you must have a way to order books."

"How thoughtful." Did she worry Lydia and Joel were too backward to care for Samy? Carl Talbert's words echoed in her mind. "I taught school for nine years before starting my own business. I use a few different book suppliers, so I'm sure I can find these. Any recommendations you can provide are appreciated."

"Even though I never saw Samy before she came to you, I have spoken with Traci. She is thrilled with the progress Samy has made during her short time here." Meredith paused to smile at Samy, who bounded into the room with her painting. "My intention is not to be critical," Meredith said with emphasis.

"Thank you for saying so." Lydia gave her a smile. "We couldn't do it without your help."

"It's my pleasure, Mrs. Yoder. I'll bring Samy to your shop when we're done."

Outside, Lydia released a long breath and leaned against a porch post to support her trembling legs. She'd never had to worry what the *Englisch* thought of her way of life. The church had been her guide. What had she gotten herself into? How would she manage to please everyone?

The metal sign in the shop window clinked against the glass. Lydia flipped it over to alert passersby the business was open, since she had been unable to establish routine hours. Even so, word of mouth was spreading the news to local families.

Local women stopped out of curiosity when they saw the sign, and some returned despite her irregular hours. A schoolteacher, who drove past on her way to and from work, suggested she may benefit from tourist business in the summer months if she advertised at least a few set hours. Lydia understood the advice was sound from her experience with tourists in Lancaster. Now, she was attempting to make a habit of opening each afternoon from two o'clock until five.

With another hour to work while Samy was with her speech therapist, Lydia chose to read the material Meredith gave her. Then she'd scour catalogues for homeschool materials, as the bishop had requested.

Lydia could almost forget her life in Lancaster ever existed. Here in an almost-perfect place, where Joel gave her everything she loved most about life, the past shouldn't make a difference to her happiness. Joel was different. He wouldn't fail Samy. And she wouldn't shut her heart to a kind and godly man.

So why did she keep expecting failure at any moment?

Was the forgiveness she needed as simple to obtain as *Mamm* suggested?

"I've been thinking."

Lydia jumped and covered her heart with her hand before realizing it was Joel's voice behind her. She turned to face him. "Why do you do that?"

"What?" Joel feigned innocence.

"Sneak up on me in my own shop." A memory of their first meeting flashed through her mind. And by the wiggle of Joel's eyebrows, he remembered, too. She swatted at his arm. "What were you thinking?"

"It can't be as deep as whatever was on your mind. But I was thinking we could use a business phone. Back home in Ontario, church members often kept them in their barns or businesses. A computer was even allowed when necessary. What were you thinking?"

"Oh. Nothing."

Joel raised his brows.

"Nothing to talk about right now. I never used a computer in Lancaster. Besides, I was pushing my limitations as a woman with the bishop already."

"Your bishop now is different."

For sure. Bishop Nafziger was unlike any other she'd known. "We are more remote here. I will think on it. Why do you want one?"

"I don't want a computer. That idea was for you. The thought came to me when I realized we ought to have a better way for the *Englisch* to communicate with us for Samy."

Would the reason for a phone become a black mark against Samy with the people? An example of how the *Englisch* ways sneak among them when the church associates too closely with outsiders? "I don't want to give any reason for the church to fear Samy among us."

"Business phones are long-established as acceptable. Members even justify cell phones now. I do not think Samy can be blamed."

"Of course not. It's just, well, I guess I don't understand how your congregation works yet."

"Datt Nafziger will not see Samy as a threat to be controlled. He sees an opportunity to be the salt and light of Christ. He would say to love is never simple and will require difficult choices. But in the end, Lydia, the right choice is always love."

Lydia closed her gaping mouth. She'd never heard love applied to interpretations of the *Ordnung*. And truth be told, the newness made her uncomfortable. But she wasn't about to confess. "I will think on it."

"Well, I need a phone in the barn. You let me know if you'd like a line in here. Or if you decide you can use a computer, we'll get one."

Joel disappeared so fast, she wondered if she had said something amiss. Then she realized, he'd been talking about more than Samy or the *Ordnung*. He was referring to the two of them. *The right choice is always love.* The words echoed in his absence.

When Meredith brought Samy to the shop, her report on Samy's progress was encouraging. Other than Lydia and Meredith, few people understood Samy's words, but she was working hard at the exercises to strengthen her oral muscles for speech.

"I've worn her out." Meredith tilted her head toward Samy playing silently with her fingers. "I'd like to begin a new therapy with her using straws and whistles. The process will require you to also do the exercises with her three times a day."

"Whatever you say will work, we will do our best to make happen."

"Well, then, here's the name of the product and website where you can order it. Once it comes, I'll teach you both how to use it. You can call me with any questions." Meredith handed Lydia a small piece of paper with frayed edges from a spiral notepad.

Lydia accepted the paper and tried to will away the flush she felt rising to her cheeks. She'd have to explain again to Meredith why she didn't have a phone.

"Oh, I forgot." Meredith reached to take the paper back.

"*Nay*, I mean, no. It's all right." Lydia folded the note and pushed it into her apron pocket, suddenly glad of Joel's foresight. "We have decided to get a business phone and even a computer. I will take care of this. Thank you."

A wide smile displayed Meredith's approval. "That's great." She leaned against the door to leave. "When you get a number, I'd like to have it for my files. See you next week."

The opening whoosh of the door caught Samy's attention. She looked up, and Lydia encouraged her to say goodbye. "Eye-ee."

"Bye," Meredith called with an emphasis on the initial b-sound and was gone.

Lydia surveyed her shop. Softened with colors of fabric, textured with crafters tools, and scented by book stacks, the room beckoned her customers with plain and simple charm. A mental image of the shop invaded by cold, noisy, wiry electronics gave Lydia the shudders.

CHAPTER FOURTEEN

Sunlight streamed through the windows, promising a clear, warm Sabbath. Joel sat on the side of his bed to pray for God's will in the decision of Samy's adoption.

Their congregation alternated worship services one week and reserved the next for family and visitation. This was visitation Sabbath, and he'd likely see every member of the small New Hope church community. Joel wished Lydia wasn't so skeptical about the response of the people to their situation. Whatever had happened to cause Lydia to expect the worst, Joel prayed *Gott* would restore her hope.

A commotion from the kitchen sounded like Lydia was busy enough downstairs for two or three women. When he'd returned from morning chores, Lydia had still been gone to gather eggs in the chicken coop. He'd seen her with her egg basket when he left the barn to fill the water trough. What could take so long to gather a few eggs? From the bang of cupboard doors below, she must be feeling rushed now.

He may as well make himself of use. Joel pulled up the suspenders on his clean pair of trousers and laid his Bible back on the bedside table. He'd read again later, maybe even with Lydia before they retired in the evening.

Before he could make out her words, Lydia's chatter with Samy echoed in the stairwell. Another voice mixed into the chatter. Who would come at this hour when most folks would wait until after lunch before going out?

Joel entered the kitchen. At a glance, he recognized the luncheon table set for four and laden with cold meats, cheese, bread, and a jar he assumed held pickles. Lydia stood at the sink with her back to him. Her head turned slightly toward the direction of the living room. Joel cut his eyes in the same direction. In the doorway, with Samy on her hip, stood Rachel.

"*Goot mariye*, Joel?" Rachel greeted him.

Before he could answer with his own good morning, Lydia turned around and said, "Oh, *goot*. I was about to see if you were ready." Lydia appeared as if Rachel showed up to lunch on a regular basis.

When he was a boy, he and Abe would not be surprised to see Rachel or Sarah in their home and invited to their *mamm's* table. His life had been entwined with the family next door to the point the Yoder and Erb children felt like siblings. Then Abe began to court Sarah, and everything changed.

Joel couldn't fathom Rachel's reason for showing up here today. He'd dragged out a long courtship with her because of pressure from Abe and Sarah to do so. Then his own ambition to farm on the island had pushed him to propose marriage. He'd left Ontario angry with her when she broke the engagement. A slow realization came to him. He owed her an apology and his thanks. She'd made a painful decision, which could harm her more than himself, because she'd known the truth—they were just friends at heart.

He watched Lydia smile at Rachel as the two gathered together the last elements of the meal. Rachel handed Samy a bowl of beets and helped her put them on the table. Was time playing a strange trick on his mind? Because he could almost believe he was back in his childhood, but all grown up.

His attention shifted to Lydia. Her countenance glowed with joy. Or was it peace? He hadn't seen her at home like this since, well, ever. Was she truly happy to have Rachel in her home? Joel couldn't make sense of the change and wasn't sure what to think about it.

"I thought maybe you'd like some help." Joel stood behind his chair at the table. "Looks like you have it all under control."

After grace, the women chatted about plans for a quilting bee. Lydia's eyes lit with enthusiasm. The extra work of hosting such an event on top of all her current responsibilities didn't seem to faze her.

"I can help wherever needed, of course," Rachel said after Lydia prattled off a long list of fabrics, threads, and supplies. "I expect you may enjoy handling the actual quilting. I can plan the meal and a game or two to give weary hands a break later in the day."

Lydia reached across the table to pat Rachel's hand. "I could never do all the work alone. Before, I had Mary and our neighbors, Martha and Anna Stoltzfus. Your offer is such a blessing to me."

"*Ach,* it's nothing. It's our way, *ya*? I know Sarah will do all she is able."

A shadow flickered across Lydia's face. Joel doubted Rachel noticed as Lydia hid her feelings behind a smile a tad less genuine than the one she had worn before. Joel knew how to ease her mind. "*Mamm* will want to help. She loves to quilt."

Lydia relaxed, and Joel noted clear satisfaction in Rachel's posture. He should have guessed at Rachel's motivation for this visit. She had always been a peacemaker. Now, he had another reason to thank her. She was welcoming his *fraw* into the community as her sister ought to have done.

Her kindness increased his guilt. He'd almost married her out of selfish ambition. She'd said as much. Now, for the first time, the truth struck his conscience and stuck like a tangled barb in Amazon's mane. He'd married Lydia with the same selfish ambition. He'd married her to get his farm. He was as low as that Simeon fellow.

"Joel?" Concern laced Lydia's voice. "*Vass is letz?* Has something gone bad? The meat?"

"Nothing's gone off. It's all very *goot.*" He took a bite and chewed to prove his words.

"You look ill," she insisted and placed the back of her hand across his forehead.

He caught her hand as she withdrew it. He might lose himself in the softness of her touch and the tender plea of her eyes. If Rachel were not present, he'd show her how he loved her.

He loved her.

His thoughts flew back to the auction of his grandparents' farm. *Ya,* he'd loved her even then. He'd married her out of selfish ambition, for sure, but not to get the farm. He'd wanted Lydia, and the farm was the only way to get her. He breathed relief, as though the barb loosened its grip.

"Should you rest instead of going to Abe's?" Lydia's cheeks were bright with a pink flush.

"It's not so far. I walked here and don't mind walking back," Rachel offered without looking at him.

He was behaving like a fool and had confused them both. "I'll be all right."

He stood to leave. Hitching the horses would give him a chance to adjust to this new reality. "I'll get the buggy in case we return late." He noted the relieved expression of both women when he closed the door behind him.

Alone in the barn, his thoughts continued to war inside him. He loved Lydia. Would she ever love him back?

Lydia watched Joel for a long minute. He'd opened the wide doors on either end of the barn, allowing a breeze to pass, and stood in the field beyond the opposite door calling to the horses. Lydia walked the length of the barn and waited for him. He turned and paused when he saw her, so she walked out to meet him.

Not fully recovered from the way he had looked at her during luncheon, Lydia's heart beat at a wild pace the closer he came. She'd already experienced one miracle this morning. Did she dare hope for another?

He looked down at her now. Horse tethers in one hand, he raised the other toward her hair. She couldn't count how many times he'd whisked the stubborn hair from her cowlick back under her bonnet. This time, he didn't remove his hand. His thumb drifted along her jaw and pressed a gentle finger against the tremor of her lower lip. He'd almost kissed her in the laundry room the other day. Was he going to finish what he started now?

"Lydia?"

She was powerless to deny the unspoken request in his voice. He wouldn't hurt her.

His forehead touched her own. "Just one. One kiss. I won't take another until after you do the asking." His voice was hoarse.

Samy was safe with Rachel. Nothing bad would happen, Lydia assured herself. She wasn't making the same mistake over again. And Joel was so different, so *wunderbaar goot.*

Her hands wrapped around the back of his neck. His black hair, softer than she had imagined, slid between her fingers.

Joel's lips covered hers with the tender affection she cherished in him. She felt him begin to pull away and lifted up onto her toes to press closer. His kiss deepened, and then he released her, though he moved no more than a mere breath from her face. "You're not making my promise any easier to keep."

All she had to do was ask for another, and he would comply. And she knew the next time he would kiss her as a man kisses his *fraw*, not a shy *maydel*. The temptation to return her mouth to his made her feel anything but shy.

Joel cleared his throat. His warm palm slid beside hers, and his fingers gave a gentle squeeze. Lydia was sure she'd be asking for more soon.

Recalling his odd behavior at lunch, she asked, "Do you mind Rachel and I becoming friends?"

"*Nay*, I was happy to see you enjoying her company."

"Maybe I shouldn't have agreed to host a quilting without first discussing it with you? But I hated to disappoint her, after all the nerve it must have taken for her to come." Rachel had found Lydia in the henhouse that morning and offered her friendship. She assured Lydia she had no intentions toward Joel and wanted to be friends.

"I am glad for you. Rachel has always been quick to make peace."

"You weren't upset with me, then?"

"I think the answer is obvious, don't you?" His eyes dropped his gaze to her lips and then to her cheeks. "You look a little flushed."

Lydia pulled her hand from his grasp and gave him a push. He came back with a nudge to her shoulder with his. If Joel ever declared he loved her, she'd be wholly unable to stop a complete freefall into love with him. She accepted he was not in love with Rachel, but did he love her?

CHAPTER FIFTEEN

Days after her first kiss with Joel, the memory still made Lydia smile. Even now, as she drew a hoe through the straight rows of her bean crop to uproot any stray weeds, her thoughts wandered, and her cheeks flushed. She was sure she'd seen Joel reliving the same thoughts. And if he hadn't placed the burden on her to ask for the next kiss, she was sure he would have repeated the act by now.

But she hadn't conjured the boldness to ask. *Nay*, instead she stayed busy. And on the farm, there was never a shortage of work to be done.

The small garden beside the house yielded bushels of tomatoes for canning, green beans, and potatoes. Now the dry bean crop promised more stores for the winter to come. The quilting bee was planned to be held after the harvest and before wedding season commenced.

Finishing her final chore of the morning, Lydia performed a mental check of her to-do list. She should have enough time to finish cutting the fabric squares she'd measured the previous day.

"Come, Samy. Let's take Yo-yo his lunch."

If Meredith heard the mispronunciation, she'd ask Lydia to model the correct form of Joel's name instead. She tried to follow the therapist's advice as much as possible, but even *Datt* Nafziger referred to Joel as Yo-yo in front of Samy now. Lydia had a deep suspicion the nickname would stick. Besides, the use of it lit Joel's face with a smile every time.

After retrieving the basket packed earlier with lunch items and a blanket, Lydia walked to the far end of their hundred-acre farm while

Samy galloped in circles around her. Joel asked her to bring him lunch if she had time. He mentioned seeing her and Samy would do him good in the middle of his day. He had been working in the far fields and taking a packed lunch with him most days to save time. Lydia couldn't deny she missed Joel coming in from work at lunchtime. She was looking forward to their little picnic. Joel lifted his hand and waved at them. By the time they reached him, he'd stopped plowing and waited under the shade of a tree. He wiped his face and neck with a handkerchief.

Samy ran into his outstretched arms.

"I'm going to get her clothes muddy," Joel said.

"No matter. A little dirt will wash." Lydia reached into the basket and felt the cool, plastic bag where she stored a wet cloth. "I did bring this for your hands before you eat."

"*Danki.*" Joel put Samy down and wiped his hands, then walked onto the blanket Lydia spread on the ground. "I could eat a horse. How about you, *liebling*? Are you hungry?"

Samy's eyes grew wide as saucers. She gaped at Lydia and then off to Amazon grazing in a far pasture.

"Yo-yo meant he is very hungry." Lydia tried not to laugh. "No one will eat the horse."

Joel was watching Lydia with a barely concealed smile. And a satisfied little girl was retrieving sandwiches from the basket. "Samy's a big girl, Lydia; you must be pleased with such fine help."

"I couldn't manage without her." Lydia played along with Joel, knowing he intended the message for his little girl.

Samy beamed under the praise and handed Lydia a wax paper package containing a cucumber sandwich. "Ee go, *Mamm*."

Lydia almost fell the rest of the way to a sitting position. Did she hear correctly? Had Samy called her *Mamm*?

Her first real word!

A glance at Joel's open mouth and wide-eyed stare in Samy's direction answered the question. She looked back at Samy. Her throat tightened, so that she couldn't respond. Lydia pulled Samy onto her lap and kissed her forehead.

"P-a-ee." Samy drew out the two vowel sounds, placed her palms together, and bowed her head. Pray. Clearly, Samy had no need for sentimentality. It was time to eat.

Joel dipped his head in a prayerful attitude, but his eyes looked up into Lydia's. If Samy's words had rendered her mute, Joel was making her breathless speaking nary a one.

If she closed her eyes in prayer, she could escape his penetrating gaze. But she didn't want to end the celebration hovering between them. Sharing this pivotal moment for a child precious to them both was clearly a victory he felt as keenly as she.

Prayer time was over according to Samy, who chewed on a huge mouthful of bread. Joel tucked into his own with a half-grin still visible. Could the very two things she never believed possible be coming true?

She'd fought to prevent placing herself in this position. Yet, she felt gloriously happy about losing.

Joel quit the fields early in order to meet the technician coming to install a phone in the shop. His lunch with Lydia and Samy replayed once again in Joel's mind.

He reflected back on the joy he'd seen in Lydia's eyes after Samy called her *Mamm*. He rehearsed again the wisdom of not kissing her, despite the desperate pull he'd felt. He would keep his promise to wait until she asked. At times, he believed she would if they were alone. *Continue to bind our hearts together, Lord.*

Today, he found assurance their time would come. If only the patience to wait for it had come, too.

He'd only returned to the barn for a few minutes when a woman came to install the phone. He felt far more at ease when Lydia arrived just after the technician began her work.

"What is that?" Lydia pointed to the laptop Joel had tucked under his arm.

"I thought I would surprise you; but since you're here, we can figure it out together." Joel sat the laptop on the counter, along with the battery pack. "You mentioned not being thrilled with the intrusion of a large computer and wires, so I asked around and found this option that should store easily in a drawer."

A smile bloomed on Lydia's face. She looked as if she was about to hug him, but quickly put her arms back down by her side. "You think of everything. Absolutely everything." Her fingers brushed across the chrome top then she flipped the top open with her thumb. "Do you know how to use it?"

Joel shook his head.

She shut the lid and drummed her fingers on the top. Her lips bunched up in thought.

"As you know, I think of everything." Joel reached into a box on the floor and pulled out a book with a black and yellow cover, *Computers for Dummies*. He laid the book in front of her. She laughed and reached out to punch him in the arm. He dodged it and laughed along with her.

The woman wiring the phone cleared her throat. Her eyes darted from Lydia to Joel and back to Lydia again. "I could help. If you'd like, that is. I could at least get you started."

Joel left the two women with their heads bent over the computer. If he ever had to use the thing, Lydia could show him what to do. He headed to the house, where Meredith would soon be finished with Samy's therapy. The mail truck was just pulling away from the box, so he sprinted the fifty yards to the end of the drive to retrieve the mail.

Sorting out the junk mail, a letter from Lydia's sister-in-law appeared to be the only significant piece of mail. Then out from a sales flyer, an envelope fell to his feet.

Child Services was marked as the sender. He could wait to open it when he always did after supper, only curiosity got the better of him. Joel slid a finger under the top to break the seal and pulled out a single sheet of paper—a summons to appear before a judge concerning the placement of Samy in their home.

Everything was going right, up to the moment he opened the notice from Child Services. How could everything turn wrong so fast?

Joel willed himself to calmness. There was a mistake or a misunderstanding. He'd clear it up. *Gott* would help him. Wouldn't He? *I need more faith, dear Lord. This is a mighty blow.*

His pace turned into a flat-out run to the house. He had to see Meredith and attempt to make sense of the notice before Lydia heard of it.

"Meredith." Joel called out before the door clicked shut behind him. Willing the panic from his voice, he called again. "Meredith, it's Joel."

No answer.

He ran to the living room, where Samy sat blowing into a whistle that looked like a party favor. Meredith was counting out loud and held a finger up to Joel to wait. At the count of twenty, Samy sucked in a breath, and the paper whistle curled back into a spiral.

"Good job. That's your last one. You can pick a sticker from the pad now."

Anxious to take advantage of the pause in Samy's lesson, Joel stepped forward and held out the letter. "I'm hopeful you can make some sense out of this for me." He looked toward Samy, meaning to indicate to use discretion. But seeing her there, playing with her hard-earned sticker rewards, his throat closed up. How long would she be allowed to remain? Content. Happy. Loved. Why would anyone take that from her? Why?

Meredith's eyebrows pulled together with concern, yet he hadn't managed to say another word. She reached for the letter. He watched anxiously as she read, as though by some miracle the words might change on the page in her hands.

He knew no such thing had happened as the crease in her brow grew deeper. She didn't even look up to him but over to Samy. And he saw the strain she was trying to hide.

"I don't know what I can do, Mr. Yoder. I can offer you and Lydia the best possible character references. I'm a first-hand witness of how Samy has flourished under your care; perhaps my opinion will hold some weight. Perhaps . . . " She sounded less than convinced of her importance in the matter. "Perhaps, it is nothing. I'm sure the court will come to the decision that is best for Samy." She sounded even less convincing than before.

"Thank you." Joel looked at his feet. What could he say?

The letter came into view. She was returning it and looking straight at him now. "We may not be of the same faith, but I believe we serve the same God, Mr. Yoder. He is a God of miracles. And He loves Samy even more than we do." She ripped a piece of paper from her clipboard and jotted on it with a pencil. "This is the name and number of a friend of mine. He's a good lawyer and child advocate; you'd be hard-pressed to find anyone who could beat him."

Joel took the paper. He hoped the time had not come for a lawyer. He knew they would need one for the actual adoption, but his prayer had been for the proceeding to go as peacefully as possible.

Meredith said her goodbyes and set a time for her next visit. Samy put her arms up to him to be held. Pulling her up to his one side, he put down the paper and looked at the name Meredith gave him.

Carl Talbert. The very man Joel suspected was at the root of the problem.

Lord Gott, we need a miracle, for sure.

Lydia was going to have to purchase Wi-Fi, a router, and an internet provider, according to Leigh, the helpful cable technician. She assured Lydia all the necessary wiring could remain in the barn and out of sight. Leigh called the arrangement *wireless,* which was the only appeal of the idea, as far as Lydia was concerned. Joel needed his tractor and mechanized farm equipment; however, the internet encompassed a whole new level of worldliness beyond Lydia's comfort zone.

"I'll have to discuss this over with my husband." Lydia studied the technician's reaction in hopes she hadn't offended her after all her effort and kindness.

"I get it." Leigh held out a small business card with her image in the upper corner. "Here's my number. Let me know. I'll waive the additional service fee to come install it for you."

Grateful for the understanding, Lydia took the card. "Thank you for all you've done today."

The bell over the door jingled.

Leigh gave a nod. "You must have a customer. I'll get out of the way. You know how to get a hold of me. Call anytime if you have questions."

Lydia looked up to see Meredith but no Samy. Meredith came closer. "I wonder if we can talk." She looked over her shoulder at Leigh. "In private."

"No problem." Leigh clearly heard the remark. "I've got to pop into the barn for a minute; then I'll be on my way." She smiled at Lydia on her way out the door.

With her focus back on Meredith, Lydia wondered at the cause of the therapist's concern. "Is Samy all right?"

"Yes, she's with Joel. My concern is over the letter you received to appear in court regarding an issue of Samy's placement in your home. Do you know of anyone who has voiced a reason for her not to remain in your care?"

"*Nay,* no. What is going on?" Lydia didn't understand what Meredith was saying. "What letter?"

"I didn't realize you and Joel had not talked about this. I'm sorry." Meredith pressed her lips together.

"Please, tell me." Lydia heard the panic in her voice. She willed herself to remain in place and hear an explanation when she wanted more than anything to run and prove Samy was still safely in the house with Joel.

"I'm sure there's nothing to fear." Meredith sounded less than convinced herself. "Court appearances are nothing uncommon within the foster system. In this case, the judge has ordered you to meet with him in order to answer some questions he has regarding Samy's placement here. I wondered if anything had happened or anyone had said something to cause a question in his mind."

"Nothing has happened. I have never even met a judge." Lydia willed away the fear threatening to overwhelm her, so she could think. "One man made some comments, but he has never seen Samy or our home. We were in a restaurant. Traci Holbrook saw us there, and this man was with her. He spoke as if he disapproved of a non-Amish child being in our care." Joel had worried about the man, even talked to Cait about him. What was his name? "Carl Talbert."

Meredith's eyes grew wide. "I see."

"You know him then."

"Yes, I hoped he might help you." Meredith eyed the new laptop on the counter. "The appointment isn't until October; perhaps I can help you with some research between now and then. The more you know about meeting Samy's needs, the better."

"Excuse me, Meredith, but I have to catch Leigh before she leaves." Lydia ran for the door and breathed a little easier when she saw Leigh's van still in the drive. Maybe Wi-Fi could be installed today, after all.

The implications of Meredith's questions and the order to see the judge hit Lydia after Leigh left with all the requested equipment installed.

Someone was trying to take Samy away. Why?

CHAPTER SIXTEEN

Bishop Nafziger called a special meeting of the area church after the traditional Sabbath service. Rumors and questions, along with untold numbers of opinions, ran amuck among the neighbors as word spread about the upcoming court appointment. Joel wished he were seated beside Lydia rather than on the opposite side of the room with all the men. He stole a glance in her direction. She sat sandwiched between *Mamm* and Rachel with Samy on her lap.

"As you are aware, members among our brethren are facing a serious trial of their faith within their home." Bishop Nafziger's words pierced Joel's heart. The members in question were himself and Lydia. The home was his own. Wrapped in the bishop's language, Joel's circumstance became more ominous than he'd allowed himself to believe. "Today, we will gather around them and pray for *Gott's* will to be done in their home and in the life of little Samy."

Menno Wagler, a dairy farmer with three teenage sons, raised to his feet. "Some of us are concerned how this will affect our community as we are new here. I'm not blaming Joel for anything. I mean, we ought to also pray for the reputation of the church to remain as one of peace and light." He said no more and sat down.

"Does anyone else wish to speak before we pray?" Invitation, rather than censor, laced *Datt's* tone.

Saul Beiler stood. "What of the use of Wi-Fi? I hear this brought the internet among us. I'm inclined to agree with the *Englischers* that Amish parents and non-Amish children should not mix."

A small gasp echoed from the women's side of the room. Joel immediately knew Lydia was both shocked and embarrassed. She'd feared this reaction. She'd acted hastily in agreeing to the Wi-Fi and regretted the decision. Joel didn't think she should have to face the issue at this moment. They'd already decided not to keep the service.

Datt's facial expression hardened. "This is not a discussion of the *Ordnung*. Those questions are to be brought to me in private and will be decided by our ministers when they are chosen. We will do all things decently and in order."

Saul was seated but appeared none too satisfied with his mouth pressed firm in a grimace.

A voice behind Joel rang out, "We are required to care for the poor, the widowed, and the fatherless. I say we pray together for Joel and Lydia Yoder. The rest is in *Gott's* hands."

Murmurs of agreement rippled throughout the room. The bishop called Joel, Lydia, and Samy to the front, where the people gathered around them in prayer. Peace washed over Joel from the power of their silent agreement, and then he noticed the rigid fear in Lydia's stance beside him.

Pretending her heart wasn't breaking, Lydia helped Samy dress for the court appointment.

Why had she believed she was worthy of this perfect life? Now, she had to watch with pain and uncertainty over Samy's future. The thought of Samy being taken away and placed in an institution was more than she could bear. Joel didn't understand why this was happening, but she did. She wasn't fit for motherhood. Even if no one else knew, she knew. *Gott* knew.

Joel called for a taxi to take them to Cardigan to meet with the lawyer. Samy was unhappy when Lydia refused to allow her to wear an apron. Lydia felt it best if she appeared as non-Amish as possible, even if she was wearing homemade clothes. Lydia wondered if the judge might appreciate how much effort was spent on making dresses for a little girl who had been delivered to the Kings with no more than the clothes on her back.

Why speculate? She had already been judged and found wanting.

Traci Holbrook met them outside of the judge's office. She looked tired with a cell phone in one hand and a tall paper cup filled with a steaming beverage in the other. By the time they were called to see the judge, Traci had downed her drink and tossed the cup into a trash receptacle. When they entered the judge's private office, they needed no introduction to the man already seated in front of the judge.

Carl Talbert sat straight in a crisp, black suit. His collar and tie appeared so tight, Lydia wondered how he could breathe. His brown hair was slicked back and shiny from whatever hair product he used. Lydia had to force her lips to smile at the man.

Beside her, Joel nodded, held out his hand in the *Englisch* way, and said, "Good morning, Carl. Nice to see you again."

Lydia wasn't sure how Joel stood at such clear peace with the man who caused him so much grief. Her own smile felt false.

If she was as good as Joel, they wouldn't be here. Suddenly, she felt as guilty as Carl Talbert for Joel's agony. After all, she was the one who was unfit for motherhood. She was the one being punished.

"Please be seated." In his long black robe, the judge motioned to the remaining chairs in front of his enormous desk. For a moment, all of Lydia's thoughts were captivated by the man's height. She imagined he must need to duck his white-haired head to get through the door. To her surprise, Lydia found his demeanor non-judgmental, rather than as imposing as his size.

Once everyone was settled, the judge began by speaking to Samy, who could not answer him. Traci intervened on her behalf, explaining the child's nonverbal condition and offering documentation of her progress through speech therapy. The judge questioned Ms. Holbrook on the special needs Samy's care would require. Mr. Talbert concurred, adding that the child required an official diagnosis from a physician or psychiatrist.

"Mr. and Mrs. Yoder, do you have any religious beliefs that would prevent you from accommodating this child's medical diagnosis, appointments, and therapy?" the judge asked.

"We do not." Joel's voice was clear and calm. "We have already installed a phone and computer in order to help meet those needs."

Mr. Talbert leaned forward in his chair closer to the judge. "While this is a commendable compromise, and no one is undermining the Yoders' efforts nor the physical fitness of their home, there is still the matter of religion to be taken into consideration."

What did that mean? Did Mr. Talbert suppose only non-religious people should foster or adopt children? The Kings had fostered for years and lived according to a deep faith. Surely, they were not being questioned because they were Amish.

"Yes, yes. I have heard you, Mr. Talbert." The judge looked again at Joel and Lydia. "I have asked you here to ascertain the facts. My intention is only to put to rest a few simple questions. Please do not be alarmed." For a brief moment, the judge's tone had softened. Lydia caught a glimpse of the man more as a grandfather than the harsh judge of her expectations.

"We will answer to the best of our ability," Joel answered.

After being assured Samy would be allowed to decide matters of faith by her own free will, the judge nodded in satisfaction. When he reached to close the file in front of him, Mr. Talbert spoke up. "I would like to request an observation period. As this type of situation has not occurred in our jurisdiction, I believe a trial period of sorts is in order."

The judge leaned back in his large, leather armchair. He faced the ceiling for a moment. And Lydia saw what appeared to be an eye roll. "Six weeks, Mr. Talbert, six weeks. At the conclusion of which, I request I hear no more from you on this specific matter so long as nothing of predicated significance is observed."

"Yes, Your Honor."

Lydia was unsure exactly what had just happened, but it seemed they'd been put on trial.

"Your Honor." Lydia mimicked the language used by the lawyer and gathered courage from the glimpse of the powerful man as a grandfather-type figure. "What are we to expect now?"

He rewarded her with a gentle and patient tone to his answer. "Ms. Holbrook will inform you of your rights. Your privacy will not be imposed upon. Let me reiterate that neither you nor your husband have been accused of any wrong-doing." His eyes shifted in the direction of Mr. Talbert. "And no evidence of such has been presented to this court."

Mr. Talbert looked down and shuffled his papers. Then, the judge returned his attention to Lydia. "Ms. Holbrook or her representative will be permitted a scheduled, hourly appointment to observe Samy in your home once a week for the next six weeks. Her observations will be documented and presented to the court, after which my final decision will be given. Does this answer your question?"

"Yes. Thank you, Your Honor."

Joel's warm hand enclosed hers.

The judge stood. "You are all dismissed."

CHAPTER SEVENTEEN

Outside the judge's chambers, Traci Holbrook pulled Lydia aside to speak to her. Her eyes gave away a sadness and worry.

"Carl is a not a bad person, Mrs. Yoder. He does believe he has the best interest of Samy at heart. I hope you can find a reason in your heart to pray for him. If he knew you as I do, he would understand Samy belongs in your family."

Lydia's own pain and confusion suffocated her. How was she supposed to carry Traci Holbrook's concern as well? She shut her eyes and leaned against the corridor wall in an effort to stem the tide of emotion.

"I'm asking for too much. I see that now. I only hoped knowing he was a good person at heart might give you hope." Traci's words were softly spoken.

Lydia opened her eyes to see Joel watching Mr. Talbert exit through the judge's door.

"I will pray for him, Traci." After all, wasn't she supposed to pray for her enemies, as the Lord commanded? But it wouldn't be easy.

"Mr. Talbert." Joel stepped up beside the man. He had his attention, eye-to-eye. "I appreciate your concern for Samy's welfare. And I was thinking maybe you would like to visit the farm. See what Amish life is like. You are welcome anytime. And my wife makes a mighty fine fried pie." Joel offered a handshake as he had done before the hearing.

A lifetime of training and habit led to Joel's instantaneous reaction. The moment was prime for the demonstration of the true Amish belief in loving one's enemies.

The stiff, formal air that surrounded Carl Talbert throughout the proceedings gave way. His shoulders relaxed, and the corners of his mouth tipped upward. "I may have to take you up on that. I have yet to experience your famous and elegant Amish cuisine."

"I've never heard our humble home-cooking referred to as elegant, but I agree it is as delicious as you will enjoy anywhere." Joel looked over at Lydia to see if she was ready to leave. Samy wiggled her way out of Lydia's grasp and ran to him with her arms up.

"Yo-yo." Samy's face lit with an adoration that would melt any man's heart. "Up." When Joel lifted her up, she buried her head into the space below his shoulder, just her size.

"I'll be seeing you." Carl Talbert's posture stiffened, and he retreated down the hallway behind them. The click of his hard-soled shoes faded into the distance with him. The sound sent chills up Lydia's spine.

If she were as pleasing to *Gott* as Joel, then this may not be happening. She wasn't, and the insidious poison of guilt surged with a deadly strike at her heart.

The taxi ride home lasted twice as long as the same route to the courthouse that morning, at least to Lydia. Joel made small talk, but Lydia's answers were short. Soon, he'd settled into silence, and Samy fell asleep.

Lydia hated the sullenness enveloping her. Was it guilt? Her sins and secrets had finally caught up to her. How had she let herself believe loving Joel would go unpunished? How had she imagined Samy might be her daughter? And now, the two people she'd come to care for most in the world might be separated from each other because she was unworthy of them. If their hearts were broken, Lydia couldn't live with herself.

The warmth of Joel's hand touched the back of her shoulder. She flinched. She felt his hand drop back to the seat beside her. Asleep in her lap, Samy shifted. Lydia refused to cry. To be vulnerable was to set herself up for more failure. She'd failed enough.

Give it to Me.

Lydia slammed the door to her heart shut. She couldn't talk to *Gott*. Not now.

When she'd confessed her past to Joel, he'd understood. He hadn't condemned her; and for the first time, she'd thought forgiveness may be possible. She should have told him from the beginning. Maybe then, they wouldn't be in this predicament.

Her mind drifted to a time before tragedy scarred her heart—to her first glimpse of Simeon Glick.

Early spring had brought a new family and their eldest son, Simeon, to Millers Creek. During most Sunday singings, Lydia stayed home with her sister, Louise. She was only in the eighth grade and too young to go courting; but on occasion, she was allowed to enjoy the fellowship with other young folks at the singing.

Chatter among the girls gathered around a bonfire in the Stoltzfus' backyard came to an abrupt end. Lydia turned her head to see the cause. A sandy-haired young man, whom she later learned was sixteen years old, joined the group of boys on the other side of the fire.

As soon as he was seated, the whispers began. And the silly talk among the girls of catching his attention caused Lydia to determine to ignore him altogether. The more she ignored him, the more Simeon Glick became determined to gain her attention. In the end, she gave him more than her attention. She vowed her heart and love to him. To him she'd been no more than a conquest. Then, he'd returned her heart in no condition to be of use again. Even now, when she finally desired to give it to another.

If only she had trusted her first instinct.

If only she had known Joel Yoder first.

The silky softness of Samy's red curls wove through Lydia's fingers. Without turning her head, she knew Joel was watching her. Her heart ached with a sadness more powerful than Simeon's memory. She once thought no misery could compare to the loss she'd already suffered. She was wrong. Nothing compared to the thought of losing Samy or Joel.

Joel had offered her grace and forgiveness when he learned her secret. If Carl Talbert ever found out, he most certainly would not.

Joel paused outside the bedroom door where Lydia had gone to put Samy to sleep. Lydia shared the room with Samy but always returned downstairs. Tonight, she stayed in the room. He hesitated to knock.

If Carl Talbert was difficult to understand, Lydia's reaction was more so. The taxi ride home was quiet. Lydia faced the car window most of the drive. Thinking back to the judge's office, Joel had wondered at her quiet resignation. One of her most admirable qualities was her determination to defend others. So, why did she appear resigned to accept defeat in this case?

He'd waited all day, in order to have a private moment without Samy listening. They needed to face this hurdle together, and that must begin with actually talking to each other.

If she wasn't coming out of the room, he'd have to get her attention somehow. His knock was almost inaudible, but he didn't want to wake Samy. When Lydia didn't answer, he pushed the door open a crack. She lay curled up beside their little girl. Joel's heart hammered in his chest. *Ya, Samy was their girl.*

Still in her dress and prayer *kapp,* Lydia's eyes were closed in sleep. Hovering near, he whispered, "Must I carry you again?"

"I wouldn't mind," her sleep-filled voice answered.

Good to know after the cold shoulder he'd received all day.

"I think you'd sleep better if you put on your night clothes." Joel paused, but she only shifted and uttered a slight groan. The pretend slumber didn't fool Joel. "Unless you want me to do that for you."

She propelled herself from the bed. Her eyes opened wide and her hand at her throat created a picture he'd not soon recall without a laugh.

"Well, then, since you're fully awake, how about joining me downstairs for a bit?" Joel turned and left the door open for her to follow, whenever she finished throwing ice-dart stares at him.

Joel had never been much good in the kitchen, but he had learned to mix a decent hot cocoa. He heard the stairs creak under Lydia's footfalls while he set a pot on the stove and poured in the milk. When he turned to the cupboard for the sugar and cocoa, Lydia was watching with a hand on her hip.

"You reckon to sweeten up to me with a hot cocoa, Joel Yoder?"

"If that's all it would take, Lydia, I'd be your hot cocoa maker every night."

She plopped down onto a chair at the table. The ice in her glare began to melt. And Joel decided to keep his mouth shut long enough to permit a complete thaw.

With his back to her, he whisked the sugar and cocoa into the warm milk and continued to stir. Once a froth developed on top, he dipped out two full mugs and dropped a handful of mini marshmallows into each steamy brew. Still unsure how he was going to get her to open up, Joel handed Lydia her hot cocoa.

Lydia looked up from her mug and met Joel with a plea in her eyes. Whatever she wanted from him, he'd give it. Didn't she know? He'd do anything to release her from the ache and pain she carried.

They sat for several long minutes. The cocoa cooled. He watched Lydia's indecisiveness twist her mouth as she started to speak and stopped. He heeded an inner warning not to push her. He waited with his hands wrapped around his cup to keep from touching her.

"I want to be free, Joel." The words finally spoken stopped his heart. "I was so foolish . . . and selfish. I made terrible choices, and the consequences never end. How could I vow my heart to someone so easily? I should never have done it." She looked up to him.

Free from her vow? To him? This was not supposed to happen. He couldn't allow it. Did she want a divorce? Terror seized his breath. He couldn't speak, but she had to see his agony.

"We made our vows before *Gott*, Lydia. I cannot, will not, go back on them. Not ever."

"*Nay, nay*, not my vow to you!" Lydia came to life with an urgency lacking in her demeanor all day. "I vowed to Simeon Yoder to never love another. And though it means naught to him, somehow the vow still binds me."

"You love him, even now?"

"No, I don't mean that." Her head bowed. "I'm doing a terrible job of explaining." Her lips pressed together tightly.

"I'll keep listening. I want to understand."

After a long hesitation, an explanation began to spill out of her as unstoppable as a waterfall. "I want to give you all you deserve, but I can't. I wish I had never been so careless with my heart. And now, when I want more than anything to be able to give it freely, something holds me back. I don't understand. Is it the vow? Does *Gott* hold me to such foolishness? I'm making no sense, but I just can't seem to overcome what was done so long ago. It was so long ago, and I'm sorry for it still."

"*Gott* does not wish to condemn you, Lydia. He offers forgiveness and peace. All we have to do is ask." If only he could make her believe this was not all her fault. But he could not.

Only the Lord could restore Lydia's heart. Joel could only continue to love her. He believed love was always the right choice. Now more than ever.

The day's events remained unresolved. The future had never appeared so uncertain to him. And he'd never needed Lydia as much as he did now. He'd forsake the farm and every other dream he'd ever had, if necessary, to hold his family intact.

"*Kumm.*" Joel lifted Lydia to stand with him. "I want to show you something."

Lydia followed Joel to the third floor and entered the top level of the round tower, called a cupola. He reached to the ceiling, and a folding staircase creaked downward, as a gaping hole to the sky opened above them.

"We can climb out onto the roof." Already halfway up, Joel motioned to her. "It's safe. I've been up here before." He looked down at her. "You've never seen a view like it. *Kumm.*"

With a sigh of resignation, Lydia filed up behind him. A gentle breeze touched her *kapp* as her head cleared the opening. Looking to the left and to the right, the low evening light revealed farms and hamlets as far as the eye could see.

She remembered a Psalm Joel read the evening before. *As far as the east is from the west, so far hath he removed our transgressions from us.*[5] She climbed up and sat on the adjacent rooftop next to Joel.

"Are you frightened?" Joel asked.

"I shimmied up trees as high when I was a girl."

Joel laughed. "I'm not surprised at all."

"My *mamm* was when she caught me. Why aren't you?"

"You've been full of courage since I've known you, Lydia. From the first time I saw you and your face set in determination at the auction, I've admired you." His hand reached over and lay over top of hers pressed tight against the sticky, black roof tiles. "I need your strength now, Lydia. I do not believe all hope is lost for Samy. You cannot either."

She dared a glance at his face, and his sincerity became her undoing. She'd been wallowing in self-pity, while Joel needed her, too. He loved Samy as deeply as she did. "I've always believed I'd choose differently if I could go back. Here I am choosing selfishly again."

"I didn't say that, Lydia."

"I know. I know you didn't. The truth is, I have to change the way I make choices if I want my life to be any different. I can't hide

---

5 Psalm 103:12, KJV

behind the past." Beulah Yoder's letter no longer remained tucked in her inner pocket, but the final words were committed to her memory. "To love as *Gott* loves is always the right choice. That's what your *gammi* said in her letter. I almost think she was talking to me instead of you."

Joel leaned backward until his back lay against the slant of the roof. "She ended every letter with those words. I hear them in my mind to this day. It's not always easy advice to follow."

"I think it may be harder than not."

"*Ya.* Seems so at times."

Reaching a matching position on her back next to Joel was not the most graceful action Lydia ever attempted. She got as far as resting on her elbows would permit, but any further felt perilous. After a few minutes, her elbows hurt, and her neck ached from bending backward to see the stars.

Joel scooted under her and lowered her gently by the shoulders until her head rested on his chest like a pillow.

"Joel, would you mind if I prayed aloud?"

"*Nay*, Lydia. I won't mind."

"I mean right now. Here."

"*Ya*, I thought so."

"Will you make sure I do it right?"

"I won't judge your prayer, spoken or unspoken. Prayer is between you and *Gott*."

"I've waited an awful long time to ask for forgiveness. What if I don't do it right?"

Joel stroked her cheek and twisted the hair dangling beside her face. "Beloved, *Gott* can read your heart no matter the words you use."

"Last night, I asked Him to change my heart. Today, I thought He had abandoned me instead. He hadn't. He was doing as I asked. He was changing my heart."

"*Danki*, Father *Gott*," Joel whispered.

"Do you think it's disrespectful to pray lying here, instead of with my head bowed?"

"Maybe in this case, having a heart right with *Gott* is more important to Him than the particulars of time and place."

Unable to hold in the need to be free any longer, Lydia looked to the heavens above her. "Our Heavenly Father, I have been too proud to come to You. I see now that I cannot earn Your forgiveness. I wasn't sure You could forgive me, which sounds so foolish when I say it out loud. You can do anything. Will you cast my sin as far from me as the east is from the west? I only ask because You have promised forgiveness through Your Son. I am sorry. I am sorry for so many things. You know them all."

Warm, cleansing tears washed Lydia's face. Unlike the many tears of pain and sorrow she had shed, these poured from a heart set free. A rushing spring of gratitude flowed through her being. "Thank you, Father *Gott*. I will never forget this gift from You."

The joy flooding her soul bubbled over into laughter. Her head rolled to the side where she saw Joel staring at her with the largest grin. His eyes shone as he reached for her hand and gave a gentle squeeze.

Ach, but she could stay here under the stars beside him forever.

CHAPTER EIGHTEEN

A knock on the kitchen door alerted Lydia to Traci Holbrook's arrival. Samy's screams to go see Amazon peeled louder. Lydia knelt to eye-level. "We will go after the bread comes out of the oven. If you cry or try to sneak to the barn again, we will not go."

Samy's lower lip quivered, and she sucked in a raspy breath, but the wails ceased.

"Much better. I knew you could do it." Lydia straightened and answered the door.

"Hello, Traci." Lydia noted the concerned lines across the woman's brow.

"Bad time?" she asked, as Samy zipped between them through the open door.

Lydia reflexively caught Samy's arm to stop her flight. Kneeling once again, she spoke to Samy. "You are not obeying. You must obey *Mamm*. Do you understand?"

Samy struggled to maintain eye contact, but her head nodded in the affirmative.

"Now, we cannot go see Amazon because you chose not to obey." Lydia braced herself for the cries sure to come.

Samy turned to Traci instead. "Eez. Go."

Lydia shook her head at Traci. "She has to learn she cannot go alone. It's not safe. She has to wait for Joel or me to take her until she is older."

"I'm sorry, Samy. I have to listen to your *mamm*, too. Even I have to do what she says this time."

Bewildered, Samy looked back and forth between the two women with her little eyebrow raised. She pointed a finger to the oven.

"No, not even after the bread is done. You did not obey." The finality of Lydia's words set off the wailing cries again. Lydia scooped the girl into her arms and held her tight. The pressure often helped Samy calm sooner. "It is okay to cry when you are sad. But you cannot cry to get your way." The cries lessened in intensity and finally stopped.

Samy ran to play in the other room, and Lydia stood to meet Traci's appraising gaze.

"Every reminder will bring another round of tears. She has such a hard time letting go of an idea once it has formed in her mind." Lydia chose her next words with care, in case Samy was listening. "After supper, I will reward her with a visit." Lydia nodded toward the barn. "If I do so too soon, then the entire lesson will be in vain."

"You certainly have the patience and strong will she needs." Traci spoke in a low voice as well.

Lydia released a pent-up breath. The approval from Traci relieved her mind. So often, she questioned whether her methods were working. Samy stretched her in the area of discipline further than any of her school children had done over the years. This was Traci's third visit since they met with the judge. Each visit meant the time for the judge's decision was getting closer. Some days, Lydia experienced a confident peace all would be well; other times, the possibility of Samy being removed from their care almost paralyzed her with dread.

"I brought something for you." Traci dug around in her large shoulder bag and produced a large pencil box. On the table, she spread out a handful of the many small, round pieces in the box. "These images have adhesive backs that stick onto a board or any surface lined with this sticky material attached." Plunging her hand back into the bag, Traci produced a large roll of the re-usable self-adhesive. Taking a few of the images, she created a sentence with pictures. "You can use this to demonstrate how a task is to be done or to make a timeline for her to follow. The images allow her to use more of her senses to understand you, since the auditory sense is still somewhat confusing to her. This also gives her a way to communicate to you using words she cannot say yet."

"That's wonderful! I never would have imagined how to do something like this."

"You're welcome." Traci's smile was large and genuine. "Use these pieces with various facial expressions, and name the emotion she is feeling, such as sad, angry, happy, and so on. She will start to recognize the emotions which changing expressions represent. She's not alone in that struggle. Most children with autism have difficulty reading faces and emotions."

In the next room, Samy played quietly under Lydia's quilt frame. Traci walked over to the spot where a baby quilt for Ben and Mary's newborn lay across the frame creating a miniature tent effect, one of Samy's favorite places to be alone.

"This one is a Christmas gift for my new nephew." Lydia pointed out the blue color scheme to Traci.

"Very lovely." Traci reached out her hand, then pulled back.

"You may touch it. I'll have to wash it after I finish."

"I've heard of the legendary Amish quilt-making but never seen one so close. Your work is very fine."

"We're having a quilting bee next week. Would you like to visit and watch?"

"Really? Oh, I'd love to. I didn't think non-Amish would be allowed."

"Cait King is planning to come. For the most part, all the women will be from our church. As my friend, you will be welcome."

"I'm honored to be considered your friend, Lydia. I hope we may remain as friends, no matter . . ."

The words remained unspoken, yet the hint of their meaning spread a dark veil over the rest of the afternoon.

After supper, Joel walked with Samy and Lydia to the far pasture, where Amazon grazed. Samy held his right hand in her left and Lydia's in the other. A year ago, he walked down the path of a farm in Lancaster to convince Lydia to marry him. At the time, he hardly dared dream he'd have harvested his first year's crop on his own farm. Now, he was walking with Lydia through their own fields alongside a little *maydel* who belonged to them in heart, if not in name.

"How about we play a game called 'Do You Remember?'" Joel talked down to Samy, while keeping his eyes trained on Lydia. "It goes like this. I ask a question, beginning with, 'Do you remember?' The first to answer correctly gets to ask the next one."

"You're making this up," Lydia mockingly scolded.

"I pay, Yo-yo."

Joel winked at Lydia. She pressed her lips together to cover a laugh.

"Do you remember the name of our horse?"

"Am-on." Samy clapped her hands. "I go." She spun in a circle as if searching for a question. "Em-ba?"

Joel looked to Lydia for an interpretation, but she shrugged.

"Remember what?" Lydia prodded.

"Em-ba corn?"

"I do!" Lydia's excitement took Joel by surprise. "I remember this field full of corn. Good job, Samy; you said corn perfectly."

Samy beamed and ran off toward the fence with her apple to wait for Amazon.

Joel had never realized the skill of spoken language required so much effort. He'd always taken the ability to talk for granted. "I appreciate how hard you work with her."

"She does the work. I know she gets tired of the effort, but she hasn't given up."

"You do more than you realize, Lydia." Joel reached for her hand, and she slid hers into his. "It's your turn."

Lydia laughed. "I thought the game was for Samy."

"Nay."

"All right. Do you remember what you were doing a year ago?"

She stole his question before he got a turn. "Ya. I was convincing the most beautiful woman I ever met to marry me." Joel watched Lydia's cheeks turn pink. He wondered for the umpteenth time why he ever promised not to kiss her again until she asked him.

"My turn." Joel kept his eyes on her. "Do you remember when I kissed you?"

Lydia stopped walking, slid her hand out of his, and rested her fingers against the side of his face. "Of course, I remember the best kiss I ever had." Before Joel could pull her closer, she slipped out of reach and jogged to the fence next to Samy.

He stepped up beside her. "You're making me crazy, Lydia Yoder. One hundred percent *farukt.*" Joel thought about the lonely night ahead and wondered how many more he was expected to endure.

Lydia stood outside her bedroom, debating whether or not to cross the hall and knock on Joel's door. He was waiting for her to ask for intimacy. Well, not exactly—he was just waiting for her to ask for a kiss. However, Lydia knew the next kiss would lead to more. After all, they were married. And their last kiss, first kiss, only kiss had promised more passionate things to come.

If she knew he loved her, then she would willingly ask as he required. He might be offended if she asked whether or not he loved her. He gave her so much. Somehow, she still needed to hear the words. When he'd called her beautiful, she'd almost given in. But being the most beautiful woman he'd ever met was not the same as being the woman he loved.

A creak of the wood floor snapped in the air. A door knob rattled. Lydia froze in her spot in the middle of the hall.

"Lydia? Is everything all right?" Joel appeared in his doorway.

Her mind raced to find an excuse for standing in the middle of the hall in the middle of the night. "Did you hear a noise?" She didn't actually say she had heard one.

"*Ya,* I heard you." He was right in front of her now. Close enough to feel his warmth and breathe in his scent.

"I'm just going to double-check the doors." Lydia moved to the steps. Her previous thoughts had been much more comfortable in the safety of an empty hallway. Now, his nearness made her tremble.

Joel caught her arm. "I'll go check. You wait here." He disappeared into his room and returned with a flashlight. "What kind of noise?"

"Just a noise."

"That's not very specific, Lydia," he muttered under his breath as he moved down the stairs.

She could hear him checking each room; then he went outside. Several minutes later, he came back. "I walked the perimeter of the house and the barn. Nothing appeared out of the ordinary. All of the doors and windows are latched. I hope you can go back to sleep. There's nothing to worry about."

"I'm sorry, Joel."

"Never mind." He kissed her on the forehead, lingering longer than necessary. "All's well that ends well."

Lydia offered a weak smile and turned to go to her room, feeling something akin to a *dumm-kobb* and praying all would truly end well.

"Lydia?" Across the darkness the whisper of Joel's voice beckoned her to turn around. "If *Gott* wills for us to come together as man and wife—" Joel cleared his throat. Even with the distance between them, Lydia felt the nervousness in Joel's hesitation. A tingle of anticipation ran up her spine as he continued. "When He wills it, we will know the time is right. It will be a gift. A precious gift to us both."

Before she could answer him, the click of his door indicated Joel was already gone. As she crawled into her own bed, Lydia knew sleep would not find her anytime soon.

CHAPTER NINETEEN

The day of the quilting brought *Mamm* Nafziger, Sarah, and Rachel to the farm before sunrise to help Lydia. Excitement and adrenaline pushed Lydia through the exhaustion she already felt from preparations ahead of time.

The house and shop were both scrubbed spotless. The evening before, Lydia had measured and cut many yards of quilting thread into thirty-six-inch strips. Every needle she possessed had been threaded and knotted, ready for use. Extra gray marking pencils were set alongside a variety of stencils, as Lydia was unsure which pattern had been chosen. The women were all bringing a variety of cloth for the cutting and piecing. Batting and backing had been ordered in bulk. And finally, a large quilting frame was set up in the center of the shop and surrounded by chairs. Then, as tired as she had been, she'd barely slept, thanks to anticipation of the day ahead.

Mamm Nafziger and Rachel already busied themselves in the kitchen and unpacked food prepared ahead of time for the dozen womenfolk expected to come. *Mamm* balanced two oblong baking dishes in her hands, then set them on the stovetop.

Lydia peeked under the foil covers at the unbaked breakfast casseroles. "I can light the oven. How long do they bake?"

"I think we should put them in an hour before the others are to arrive. I just set them there to come up to room temperature before baking. Can you mix the juice?" *Mamm* passed Lydia three containers of orange juice concentrate.

Lydia stirred with one hand and measured coffee into a filter with the other. Rachel crammed more prepared casserole dishes into the refrigerator for the midday meal, while *Mamm* arranged homemade doughnuts and cookies on a platter. All the while, Sarah rocked and nursed her babe in the corner, her eagle eye honed into every movement in the room.

A chill traveled up Lydia's spine. Would the woman ever accept her? The trouble was Lydia couldn't deny Sarah had reason to be suspicious of her relationship with Joel, even if the matter was none of her business. And Lydia couldn't help but admit she would feel wounded if she and Louise had been in the same situation. Still, Lydia had a hard time believing she would ever meet approval in Sarah's eyes under any circumstance.

A rustling sound from upstairs caught Lydia's attention. "Sounds like Samy is awake." Lydia tapped the whisk against the glass rim of the juice picture, then tossed it into the hot, soapy water she'd prepared in the sink. "I'll finish this in just a minute."

With a half-hearted attempt at a smile to Sarah, whom she couldn't bypass, Lydia met Samy on the stairs and helped her to the washroom.

"That child is as wild as a barn cat. Who knows what kind of chaos she'll create at a quilting bee?" Either Sarah believed Lydia couldn't hear her in the washroom, or she didn't care.

Doing her best to ignore the stinging remarks, Lydia helped Samy wash her hands. With a comb, she gingerly untangled the red curls, parted her hair straight down the middle, and plaited each side into a tight braid behind her ears. With no time to spare, Lydia grabbed the clothes she had set in the room earlier and dressed Samy.

"There now, let's just wipe the sleep out of your eyes." Lydia reached for a cloth, and Samy reflexively squeezed her eyes shut. Lydia bent down at eye-level with Samy. "Here. You try." Lydia knew the sticky tear crystals would remain in the corners of her eyes, but the smile on her face at being entrusted with the task meant more than a clean face at the moment.

Rachel's voice carried from the other room. "As if you have any room to talk, Sarah Erb Nafziger. You turned our *mamm* gray-headed before we were school-aged."

Mamm Nafziger's laugh filled the air. "*Ya,* Belinda declares so to this day."

Lydia couldn't help but smile at the banter. Maybe she shouldn't take Sarah's words so strictly to heart, as she'd learned with Miriam Stoltzfus over the years at home in Lancaster.

"Go Yo-yo." Samy pulled on Lydia's sleeve.

Lydia was torn. Allowing Samy to spend the day with Joel would relieve the stress of keeping an eye on her during such a busy day. And yet, a strong pull to share the quilting bee experience with Samy tugged at her heart. Was this how motherhood felt?

Lydia leaned against the bathroom sink for support, her legs weak for a moment from the realization—Samy was the daughter of her heart.

Mother. Wife. No matter how carefully she'd controlled her feelings and her life, she was both. She'd run to Prince Edward Island to escape her past and landed right in the middle of her biggest fears. Lydia pushed away the nagging worry Samy would be taken from them. She couldn't dwell on her worry and get through this day.

"*Mamm?*" The little voice called Lydia's attention back to the washroom and the small hand pulling at her skirt.

Lydia bent down. Her forehead touched against Samy's. "How about we share today? You spend the morning with Yo-yo and the afternoon with me?" Lydia had to lean backward to avoid a head-butt as Samy jumped up and down with excitement.

Determination steeled her. The past was as far from her as the east is from the west. And *Gott* controlled the future.

When Joel came into the kitchen from his morning chores, he'd spoken in politeness to his *mamm* and nodded to the other women in the kitchen. He had to hurry before Lydia's quilting bee was at full swing. He headed straightaway to Lydia's desk for paper and pen, then up to his room.

Joel opened his Bible to the book of John, where he had been reading the night before. Not by happenstance—as he'd read from John each night for a week—he came to chapter eight, verse thirty-two. *And ye shall know the truth, and the truth shall make you free.* He had no doubt the Lord intended for him to share the encouragement with Lydia. His eyes plunged down the page to verse thirty-six. *If the Son therefore shall make you free, ye shall be free indeed.*

Looking down to write, he took a closer look at the paper he'd snatched from Lydia's desk. Far from being the blank sheet he'd intended to grab, the margins told a story etched in pencil along the left side and across the bottom. No words. No people. Yet all the scenes together told a story he knew by heart.

In a row down the right margin, images leaped off the page—his grandparents' farmhouse, a bench by a pond, and an auction tent. In the bottom left corner was the Confederation Bridge crossing to Prince

Edward Island. Then in panorama across the bottom margin spanned a clear rendition of their farm.

Joel zeroed in on the farm. At first glance, the shadows didn't match their objects. Then on closer inspection, Joel discovered the absence of human figures were represented in the three shadows. A narrow one trailed away from the porch. The other two, one long and one short, extended beyond the barn. Lydia's view of himself and Samy in the barn.

His chest tightened like a vice gripped his rib cage. Were these scenes as dear to Lydia as they had become to him? Hope surged through him with a power to believe as he hadn't been willing before now. Depicted in the frame was their story. Different as they may be, they were a family. His own. And how he loved them.

Taking the pen in hand, he wished he'd been more diligent in handwriting class. His scratch would likely ruin the beauty there, but the words begged to join the page.

With his heart full, Joel copied the verses as he had planned. Then below, in an act he had not forethought, he signed the note. "I love you. Always, Joel."

Deciding he needed an envelope to deliver the more intimate message than he had originally planned, Joel folded the note, slid it into his Bible, and went downstairs to find one.

An hour later, Joel realized he had never gotten the envelope or delivered the message. After being waylaid in conversation with his sister-in-law, then catching sight of incoming buggies, he'd skedaddled with Samy as fast as he could.

Hand-in-hand, they walked the fence line of a pasture soon to hold several head of steer. Along with their first milk cow, the steer were scheduled to be delivered from a nearby farm at the first of the following week, and he wanted to double-check for any potential weak spots.

Samy sang her ABC's. No one would ever convince him that his girl was anything less than brilliant. He didn't understand why she couldn't form words, but her mind was sharp. She'd memorized the song with ease. He might not be an expert, but for a three-year-old, he knew she was doing well. For some letters, she could still only make a long *e* sound. He'd never noticed before that the individual letters made two separate sounds, most beginning with a hard consonant and ending with a long *e*. "A-ee, B-ee, S-ee, D-ee . . ." Samy continued. His chest swelled with gratification for all she was learning. She got to *j* and missed a beat. He knew she would get it soon and selfishly hoped she wouldn't drop his nickname when she mastered the guttural sound. He liked being Yo-yo.

How could he endure life without little Samy? Whatever Mr. Talbert's prejudice was against them, they had done no wrong. Despite the nagging worry of the judge's power to decide their fate, Joel clung to faith in the One Whose judgment was holy and just.

Even if the decision is not what you want? The question stabbed his heart. *Yes, Lord. I will trust You, even if . . .*

"Hello there," a man's voice called from a distance.

Joel turned to see Carl Talbert crossing the field toward them with a determined stride. He wasn't wearing a suit. He was dressed like a local farmer ready to work and appeared comfortable outdoors. Joel squinted. For sure, the man was none other than Carl Talbert.

"I decided to make good on your offer to see the place."

Lydia looked around the circle of ladies, all hands in motion and moments of silence a rarity. The quilting bee was hard work, for sure, and yet something of a vacation from the usual work womenfolk performed day after day. Just like back home, the creation of a quilt provided a sense of camaraderie as they worked together.

Rachel's chair scraped against the floor as she slid back to excuse herself from the circle where she was helping the ladies basting the layers together. A glance at the clock showed the time was almost noon. How the hours had zipped past, even if Lydia's cramping fingers welcomed a rest from stitching the tiny, two-inch squares into larger, four-inch squares. The design, chosen by the older women and given to her in the preferred order, appeared random. She had yet to figure out the design.

"I'll help you," Lydia spoke to Rachel. The circle of women hovered over their work, so that Lydia could still not make out the pattern.

"Lunch should be ready by half past noon," Rachel called out and motioned for Lydia to come along. The hums of approval and anticipation made Lydia smile. What a genius Rachel was. She had known exactly how to bring this fledgling church community a sense of unity. The gift of being included was not lost on Lydia. A friend like Rachel was a treasure, indeed.

Rachel emptied apple filling from mason jars into a baking dish and sprinkled the top with crumb topping. Lydia backed away from the vegetable soup she was stirring on the stovetop, as Rachel placed the apple crumble into the oven. Everything was basically prepared. Bread and cheese were arranged on the table, and a large batch of lemonade needed to be poured into a pitcher to serve.

Lydia had an idea for another beverage, since there was time. "My garden is almost over-run with mint. I suppose the previous owner didn't know to plant it in a container."

"That wild stuff will take over."

"I think I'll go cut some for some mint tea."

"That would be *wunderbaar goot*, Lydia. I can put a pot of water to boil."

"*Danki*. Be right back."

Lydia scooped up the basket in which she kept her scissors on the porch for quick trips to gather and carry herbs and vegetables from the garden. Two envelopes lay in the basket. Joel must have gotten the mail. The top envelope was addressed from her brother's wife, Mary. Lydia popped both into her apron pocket without checking the one underneath. The letter from Mary would be a lovely treat at the end of this busy day.

Across the way, Lydia caught sight of Joel and waved. He jogged to her at the garden.

"Hello." A smile curved his mouth, and he looked at her expectantly.

"Hello." Lydia replied. Why was he still staring at her? "Do I have something in my hair or on my face?" She wiped at her face and felt for hair falling out of her *kapp*.

"You look perfect, Lydia. Did you find the letters?"

"*Ya, danki*. I'll read them this evening." Lydia was baffled by the disappointment on his face. Joel had never worried over a letter from Mary. "Is everything all right?"

"Sure, sure. How are things going with the quilting?"

"Right on schedule. Are you joining us for lunch? Samy will be getting hungry."

"I wanted to tell you to expect one more for lunch. Carl Talbert is here. He's in the barn with Samy now. He's a better hand around the farm than I would have guessed." Joel laughed without a hint of concern over the revelation that Carl Talbert was here.

"What in the world is he doing here? Today?" Lydia heart doubled its normal rhythm. Finding humor in a visit from that man was beyond her charity at the present.

"I invited him, remember? Everything is all right, Lydia. *Gott* must have a purpose in bringing him to us today." He rubbed his hand down her free arm and gave her hand a gentle squeeze.

"I will try to think of it as you say." She would have to try very hard. "Cait is coming for lunch and will join in the quilting. Traci is supposed to come as well. I suppose this is a day for *Englischers* to learn to quilt."

Joel chuckled, and a lighter mood eased Lydia's spirits. Maybe a little humor was in order after all.

Joel winked at her. "That's my Lydia."

Lydia hollered out to him as he trotted back to the barn. "We'll be ready to eat in twenty minutes."

Joel threw a thumbs up into the air before he ran fully out of sight.

His Lydia. He'd never said those words before. Lydia puzzled a moment over the emotion the words evoked. Cherished was the only description which fit. What a *wunderbaar* feeling.

CHAPTER TWENTY

Joel hung back from the crowd at lunch. The noise and chatter had begun to overwhelm Samy. He'd watched Lydia maneuver Samy around large social gatherings, helping her cope with the noise, which often hurt her ears. The porch served as a quieter space for her at the moment.

"I thought I'd find the two of you out here." *Mamm* poked her head out the kitchen door. "How about if I spend some time with Samy? She'll be needing a nap soon. The women will be heading back to the quilting, and I think you ought to go over with Lydia."

To a quilting bee? "More likely, I should go tend to a few chores, if you really can be spared for a bit."

"I can be spared, but only if you listen to your *mamm* and do as I asked." A smile tipped the edge of her mouth. "I am serious about going with Lydia. Even a grown man should know when to trust his old *mamm's* instinct."

Joel kissed her on the head. "You're not so old. I will go." Surely, she wasn't senile either.

Carl Talbert was walking toward the shop with Traci. Meredith's car pulled into the drive. She usually arrived after Samy's nap. This quilting bee had the makings of the strangest one Joel ever heard tell of.

Inside the house, Rachel dragged him toward the washroom and whispered close to his ear. "Keep Lydia here for ten more minutes. All right? Then bring her to the shop."

Was he the only sane person left? "All right, Rachel." He agreed, since the conspiracy obviously spread beyond his *mamm.* "What is going on?"

"You'll see." She grinned and darted away.

Special quilts were often made as gifts for members of the community or even as fundraisers for a family in need. He supposed Lydia was about to receive such a surprise, but he'd never witnessed men and *Englischers* roped into the quilting. Carl Talbert had been full of surprises today, but Joel had his doubts quilting skills would be among them.

Joel approached Lydia from behind, wishing she had read his note. He leaned over her shoulder, and she jumped.

"There you go again. You gave me a fright." She swatted at his arm with her dishtowel. "And you don't appear the slightest bit remorseful."

"Can't say that I am." Joel grabbed the towel before she could swing again. "Can you take a minute to check the mail I brought to you earlier?"

"Are you expecting something? I didn't look at the bottom envelope."

In a way, he was definitely expecting something. "That would be great." He followed her to her writing desk.

"It's from you!" She swung around, gave him a quizzical glance, then plopped onto a chair and opened the note.

I love you. Always, Joel.

Joel loved her!

She fingered the page on which she'd drawn a picture meant for her former neighbor, Anna Stoltzfus. She'd just been doodling and thought Anna would appreciate a letter with a picture of her new life. And then without intention, her pencil told a story too intimate to send, so she'd drawn another and sent it instead.

She folded the page and pressed it to her chest. "Oh, Joel."

He stood just a few feet in front of her. "I thought the verse might encourage you today."

The truth shall make you free.

She wanted to say more. The words were taking far too long to form into a coherent sentence.

He turned to face the window. Was he embarrassed?

"We better head on over. Everyone's been gone for a spell now. I don't want to keep you from them."

Lydia regretted not finding the right words in time. He was right, though. Everyone would be at work already. As the hostess, she should be there. By evening, she'd find the words to say when they were alone again.

Joel opened the shop door for Lydia to enter. The room fell silent. The church women stood together in front of the quilting frame. She'd begun to suspect they were all up to something.

Their sober faces almost brought a laugh, until the idea something could be wrong came to mind. Traci, Meredith, and Carl sat to one side. On the other side were Cait and *Mamm*, who held Samy asleep in her arms. Poor thing must be worn out.

Belinda Erb stepped forward. She didn't live in their community, but her husband was a minister in the Ontario church, so all the woman respected her as they did *Mamm* Nafziger. "On behalf of my daughters, Sarah and Rachel, and all the women folk of your New Hope congregation, I have been asked to welcome you into the community with this quilt. Of course, the quilting has yet to be done, but we can't keep the design a secret any longer now that it's all pieced together. We hope you like it, Lydia."

Tears pooled in Lydia's eyes as the women stepped to the sides of the frame. The design they'd worked to keep secret remained a blur in front of Lydia. Beside her, Joel handed her a handkerchief. She dabbed her eyes and stepped nearer, unprepared for the picture revealed to her.

"Samy?" How had anyone managed to transform all those tiny squares into the shape and form of a little girl? A patchwork child in a dress and bonnet with red curls framing her face graced the center of the quilt with surrounding squares in colors representative of the seasons.

"I've never seen anything like this." Lydia looked at the women. "I can never thank you enough. I'm so very grateful and honored. I will make sure Samy keeps it always."

Lydia's tears fell, despite her attempt to hold them back. Would Carl Talbert think she was trying to manipulate his opinion? She already supposed Traci and Meredith worked on him to get him here today. She took a deep breath. Several women patted her on the back.

"We'd better get to quilting," someone chimed. Chairs scratched against the floor as the women gathered around to begin their task. Their needles rocked up and down as they expertly sewed eight and nine stitches to an inch. When complete, the cover would be patterned with rows exactly two inches apart with their hand quilting.

Traci Holbrook came to her. "I'd like to stay awhile, if you don't mind. I'm fascinated by the process. I'm just going to step out with Carl for a minute. He's getting ready to leave." Traci leaned closer. "This has made quite an impression on him in favor of your community."

Lydia looked for Joel and saw him near the door with Mr. Talbert. She hadn't spoken to their guest yet and should at least say goodbye. As she came to them, Carl extended his hand toward her. She shook it. "Thank you for coming today, Mr. Talbert."

"The pleasure has been mine; I assure you." His tone was devoid of the suspicion normally present. "I believe you will be hearing from the judge soon. I plan to withdraw my complaint. In fact, I will go a step further and advocate for Samy's adoption."

Joel grabbed her hand. The women in the room gasped. A few hands clapped lightly. Traci smiled up at Mr. Talbert with approval. Everything began spinning together in front of her. He was leaving.

"Wait!" Lydia hadn't intended to shout.

"Don't go yet." Lydia stepped forward to catch up. "Mr. Talbert, I don't believe you have all the facts."

She was thankful he had changed his mind, but Lydia knew he had reason to be suspicious. She knew *Gott* had forgiven her. But if the courts knew, would they take Samy away? Lydia needed to know once and for all.

"My younger sister was killed in an accident many years ago. The police charged the drunk driver who hit her. Even though we forgave him, he went to jail. My sister was a lot like Samy, although no one ever knew about autism or why she couldn't speak to us. My father was very sick, and my mother asked me to watch her. I was fifteen and paying more attention to my beau than I was to my sister. She was killed by the side of the road playing at the mailbox. I was responsible for her that afternoon. I've always wondered, Mr. Talbert, wasn't I as guilty as the man who went to jail?" Lydia looked him in the eye. "Wouldn't you find me so and take Samy from me?"

For a moment, Lydia believed she saw pity in Carl Talbert's eyes, but then she recognized a mirror image of the pain which haunted her own eyes for so many years.

"No, Mrs. Yoder, I would not find you guilty. You were a child yourself. You made a mistake and bear the burden of a terrible tragedy." His voice wavered.

Was he living with his own personal trial, as she had?

He continued, "From what I have observed, neither you nor your husband would allow such an accident to occur, if at all within your control."

Lydia became aware of the silence around her. Everyone had heard.

The truth shall make you free.

Lydia didn't feel free. She felt like a fool for bringing up the past that had been cast as far as the east is from the west.

If the Son therefore shall make you free, ye shall be free indeed.

Carl Talbert cleared his throat and spoke low for her and Joel only to hear. "I would not find you guilty, Mrs. Yoder. However, I am now obligated to inform the judge. His verdict is the one that decides, as far as Samy is concerned. I will do my best to advocate on your behalf."

What had she done?

She'd told the truth—the truth which held her captive for almost half of her life. The possibility of losing Samy ached with the same intensity as it always had. Lydia could have kept the knowledge to herself, and Samy's adoption was all but assured. Why hadn't she? Because she didn't want the past to hover over both her future and Samy's. She wanted a clean slate for Samy, too.

The judge's decision was in *Gott*'s hands.

CHAPTER TWENTY-ONE

Joel and Lydia's one-year anniversary came with an unexpected surprise, rendering Joel's plans better than he'd hoped. As far as he was aware, she had no more startling revelations to make known to the world, so today's events should go without a hitch. Anniversary celebrations weren't common among the Amish, but Joel had an important purpose for this one.

Datt Nafziger's horse and buggy pulled up beside the barn right on time. *Datt* and *Mamm* climbed out, and Joel caught up to them. "Can you leave your overnight bag in the buggy? I don't want to give away the fact we're going for two days just yet." His parents were keeping Samy at Annandale Farm, since *Datt* had no animals other than his own horse. "*Danki*, for taking care of the farm while I'm gone, too."

"I haven't forgotten how to manage a farm yet." *Datt* gave him a stern eye, but *Mamm* laughed.

"How's Lydia supposed to pack if she doesn't know?" *Mamm* offered the warning look this time.

Joel hadn't considered that issue. "I'll give her time. Don't worry."

"Humph?" *Mamm* clicked her tongue and headed to the house. *Datt* laughed.

"Abe and Sarah are coming before you go. They wanted to say goodbye."

"What for, *Datt*? We'll be gone for only two days." So much for pulling this off without a hitch.

Datt shrugged and followed *Mamm* toward the house.

"Samy's still asleep," Joel called after them.

Joel went to the henhouse and found Lydia gathering eggs. Her expression rent his heart. Since the quilting bee two weeks ago, her smiles were weak and her eyes dim. He prayed their trip would bring back her joy.

"Happy Anniversary, *mei fraw.*" Joel avoided the rooster and met her inside the henhouse.

"You remembered." Her smile was fuller this time.

"I'm not likely to forget the best decision I've made since my baptism."

She blushed.

Joel would never tire of her blushes. "I've planned something special for us."

"Joel, I think you better leave the henhouse." Lydia nodded her head toward the door behind him.

He hadn't counted on that reaction.

"The rooster, Joel, he's not happy with you in his kingdom."

He didn't need to be told again. A rooster's spur stabbed into a calf or shin hurt worse than being thrown from a horse—in his experience, at least.

"How special?" Lydia asked, as she joined him.

"How special do you think a trip to the center north of the island and an overnight stay near the Anne of Green Gables farm might be?"

"Really, Joel?" Her arms wrapped around his shoulders, and her egg basket whacked him in the spine. "Oh, sorry." She pulled back and inspected her eggs. "Nothing's broken."

"If my back doesn't count, you mean." He winked at her. "So, I did all right in choosing a surprise?" he asked, even though her smile was all the answer he needed. "Can you be ready by nine? The driver is arriving between nine and nine-thirty."

"What time is it?"

"Sevenish."

"Two hours, Joel Yoder. You give me two hours?" She thrust the egg basket against his middle and took off in a run.

Joel followed her behind and heard the phone ring in the barn.

"Hello?"

"Yes. This is Carl Talbert. Is this Joel?"

"It is." Joel prayed the news wasn't going to ruin Lydia's trip.

"I have great news, Mr. Yoder."

Great news was an understatement. Joel managed to convince the lawyer to come tell Lydia in person before they left.

He headed to the kitchen, praising *Gott* all the way. When he walked inside, Lydia flew past like a hurricane with an iron in hand.

"Someday, you'll learn." *Mamm* gave him a pointed look.

"*Ya*, you were right, of course." However, Joel imagined surprising Lydia would always be his favorite way of doing things.

The desire to get going was like an itch Joel couldn't reach to scratch. Two hours moved like an eternity to him, while Lydia fluttered around the house, giving instructions and finding more items to pack in her bag. Joel watched out the window. If Abe and Sarah were coming, he wished they'd hurry up. He didn't want to wait after the driver arrived. The rumble of a car motor came from outside. At least Carl Talbert was on time.

"There's someone here to see us, Lydia." Joel caught her hand. "Will you come outside with me?"

She didn't ask any questions. She stood beside him on the porch, and Joel wrapped an arm behind her waist. She wobbled a little when she saw Carl getting out of his car. Maybe surprises weren't always a *goot* idea. He should have prepared her for this one.

"Hello," Joel called to Carl, who stepped onto the porch. "*Danki* for coming so quickly."

Carl shook Joel's hand, then turned to Lydia. "I am delighted to deliver this message to you in person, Mrs. Yoder. I have received the judge's determination."

Lydia swayed in Joel's arm. He held her tighter. "It's *goot* news, Lydia." Joel nodded at Carl to continue. "Best to hurry up and tell her."

"I do have the best of news. The judge respects your honesty, Mrs. Yoder. He finds your truthfulness recommends you as highly as does your admirable efforts to do for Samy what the foster system has been unable to do. That is to provide her with a secure, stable, and loving environment in which she can flourish. The court date to finalize the adoption of Samy into your family will be set for no later than the end of this year."

Joel barely caught Lydia before she landed on the floor. "Easy there."

"I just need to sit for a minute."

"I understand." Carl stepped away. "I'll be in touch."

Lydia reached out a hand toward Carl. "Don't go. I haven't thanked you."

"You've done more for me than you know, Mrs. Yoder."

"Please call me Lydia. We don't use mister and missus among the Amish, except in reference to . . . well, non-Amish."

"I'm honored, Lydia. I'll be in touch. I really must go, and I wish you many happy anniversaries to come."

The ocean view on the north side of the island differed significantly from the quiet bay in Cardigan to the east. Joel lay on a blanket behind her, while Lydia scanned the far horizon of the Atlantic. The day was too cold for the average tourist, so she and Joel enjoyed some privacy.

Lydia replayed Carl Talbert's message over and over in her mind. When she'd examined his words for the millionth time, she rehearsed the apology Sarah offered as they left.

Louise's story showed Sarah how fortunate she was to have her sister, Rachel, and shamed her for her behavior toward Lydia. She confessed to acting out of jealousy and bitterness. Lydia forgave her sister-in-law. She doubted Sarah's judgmental nature would change overnight, if ever, but she wouldn't hold the past against her. She had no right, when she had been forgiven so much herself.

Mary and Ben were bringing their family to the island for Christmas, so Lydia could meet her newest nephew. Now, Lydia could write back and tell Mary of one more addition to the family. By the time of their arrival, Samy would be a Yoder in name and in heart.

"It's getting colder." Joel came up behind her. "Maybe we should head to the restaurant."

"A little longer, *please*." Lydia wanted to relish all the joys of this day a few more moments before the noise of everyday life drowned out the pure thrill of peace flooding her soul.

Warmth enveloped her as Joel's arms wrapped around her from behind. He kissed the nape of her neck, and she shivered. "See there. You're cold." He turned her around to face him, all the while with his arms holding her close. "I'm so glad you married me." He touched his forehead to hers.

She waited for him to kiss her. He hovered so close. One hand moved to her cheek, and he traced a finger along her cheek. "Since the moment you tried to beat that buyer at his game in the auction tent, I've been falling for you. I don't know exactly when my heart became yours, but I love you, Lydia Yoder. I love you with all I am."

She thought she would burst if he waited any longer. "Will you never kiss me, Joel?"

"I thought you'd never ask."

The softness of his lips touched hers, and Lydia leaned nearer. His hand moved behind her neck and cradled her head, then pulled her into his kisses.

Out of breath and not caring, Lydia whispered the words beating in her heart. "I love you, too."

He paused in kissing her, but held her. She opened her eyes and found him searching hers. "Will you marry me, Lydia?"

"You stopped kissing me to ask me to marry you? We are married, Joel." Her nose pressed against his and a laugh bubbled out of her.

"There's a bit of a problem. The previous arrangement has become disagreeable." A smile teased at the corner of his mouth. "I'm asking for a real marriage. The marriage I'm proposing joins a man and woman as one and fills a house with children, if *Gott* wills."

"I see." Lydia looked deep into the brown eyes of the man she wanted to spend the rest of her life loving. "You're asking for an honest marriage, where the truth is told between us always. And we cherish and honor one another, no matter how difficult. Oh, and you help change diapers of smelly little *boblen*, either of our own or of our hearts like Samy."

"I will." Joel smiled wide and gave her a quick kiss. "And I will love you as *Gott* has loved me, until death us do part."

"Well, then, I will marry you, Joel Yoder."

Joel grabbed her waist and swung her in a circle. Before her giddiness eased, he scooped her legs up and held her in his arms. "Well, then, what are we waiting for?"

"You can't carry me all the way back to the inn, Joel."

He shot a defiant glare down at her. "I can do a great many things you don't know about, Lydia."

"I've no doubt." Lydia threw her arms around his neck and held on for the ride.

EPILOGUE

Alt Grischtaag, Old Christmas, 6 January, 2018
Annandale Hill, Prince Edward Island

Mary stepped out of the hired van with a chubby, golden-haired boy squirming to get out of her arms. The other children filed out, finally followed by Ben. Lydia threw her arms around them all and squeezed the older boys more than they could tolerate.

"I'm so happy you've come."

"Don't forget me." Anna Stoltzfus jumped out of the van. "I convinced them they needed a mother's helper for the trip."

"How *wunderbaar* to see you too, Anna."

Lydia hurried everyone in from the cold. "*Kumm* and meet Samy. She may be a little shy around so many new faces at once," Lydia warned. "Joel is finishing chores in the barn. He'll be in soon."

"Maybe the boys should go help and work off some energy before we let them in the house." Mary shooed the boys, who ran off to the barn with Ben close behind them.

Inside the house, Samy hid under the quilt frame until Anna coaxed her out. She was fascinated by her cousins for a few minutes, then returned to her favorite hiding place.

"Don't worry," Lydia told Anna. "Sometimes she just needs a break from the noise or too many new things. She'll come back when she's ready."

Anna nodded.

"Go ahead and show the girls upstairs. They can pick their room from the two on the third floor. The boys will get the other room."

The girls giggled with delight and ran upstairs.

"Do you think you'll ever fill up this big house, Lydia?" Mary half-teased, half-stared in wonder.

"*Gott* can do anything, I've learned. We would also like to foster more children, as we did Samy. Whether for adoption or not, so many need a loving and stable home."

Mary embraced her in a warm hug. "My heart is full to see you so happy, Lydia. How many families are here now?"

"Enough to choose a new minister. More families are set to come in the spring from Ontario. We should even be able to support a teacher and a school."

"All from Ontario but one, *ya?*" Mary smiled at Lydia. "Do you think Joel will be chosen as the new preacher?"

The idea had once filled Lydia with dread, but the past no longer held the same power over her heart and thoughts. "If *Gott* wills, then Joel will be a fair and truthful minister. He has taught me so much already."

What would Mary think of all the times Joel had read the Scriptures to her? She hoped to share with her someday.

"We miss you so much, Lydia, but you belong here. I can see the change in you. I'm so thankful to *Gott* for giving you joy again." Mary's eyes misted, and she brushed at them with the back of her hand.

Lydia put an arm around her beloved sister-in-law. As Lydia tilted her head, she felt Mary's *kapp* gently pressing into her own. For a moment, they stood side-by-side without speaking, the merry sound of girls upstairs and the stomping boots of men and boys entering the kitchen surrounding them. Lydia's heart was full.

"*Ach*, Mary. *Gott* has gathered all my tears and watered my dreams."

Dear Reader,

Thank you for reading *Forever Home*. I hope you have enjoyed your time with Lydia, Joel, and Samy on their journey to becoming a family.

The New Hope Amish community on Prince Edward Island is fictional. In fact, Canadian Amish settlers from Ontario arrived on the island in 2016, drawn by the fertile farmland at cheaper costs than were available in southern Ontario. New Hope is not intended to resemble any of those churches or their members and is purely my own invention.

The inspiration for the New Hope Amish church in *Forever Home* was born out of my experience with members of the Amish faith and their courageous question. How should a modern-day Amish community appear, while still holding firmly to the salvation message for which their ancestors were persecuted?

As a follower of Christ, I have often pondered the same question concerning my own faith. If stripped down to the essentials, what matters most? I believe the answer is the same as the conclusion reached by the Swiss Anabaptist ancestors of the Mennonite and Amish faith— salvation by faith alone through Christ alone. This one truth holds every life-transforming power. Every generation and each individual face the challenge of living a life which allows the Light of this same message to be proclaimed and received.

Forever Home is the story of how one small church and one young family seek to live this truth through the trials and circumstances in which they have been placed. My prayer is that their story may encourage your faith wherever love and truth find you.

I would love to hear from you. You can find me on Instagram, Facebook, and Twitter, or through my website, www.AmyGrocho.com.

Blessings,

Amy Grochowski

For more information about
Amy Grochowski
&
Forever Home
please visit:

www.amygrochowski.com
www.facebook.com/amygrochowski
www.instagram.com/AmyGrocho
www.goodreads.com/amygrocho
@AmyGrocho

For more information about
AMBASSADOR INTERNATIONAL
please visit:

www.ambassador-international.com
@AmbassadorIntl
www.facebook.com/AmbassadorIntl

If you enjoyed this book, please consider leaving us a review on
Amazon, Goodreads, or our website.

More from Ambassador International

A paramedic and reporter search for the truth behind their town's corruption . . . the only problem is that the truth they are hunting is hunting them.

Alabama Days
by Daphne Self

After waking up in a strange wooded area without a memory, Charlotte teams up with Nicholas and Vincent to figure out who she is and why fear and confusion won't leave her alone. Trust is awfully hard when one is so clearly confused.

Clear Confusion
by Kathy M. Howard

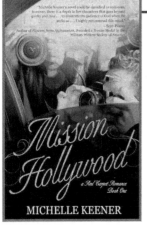

A Hollywood bad boy. A pastor's daughter. What could possibly go wrong?

Mission Hollywood
by Michelle Keener